DARK
CIRCUS

THE ASTONISHING RETURN

By: Nick Lee

"Dark Circus: The Astonishing Return" by Nick Lee. ISBN 978-1-62137-945-4 (softcover); 978-1-62137-946-1 (hardcover); 978-1-62137-947-8 (eBook).

Published 2017 by Virtualbookworm.com Publishing Inc., P.O. Box 9949, College Station, TX, 77842, US.

Chapter 1
A Familiar Breeze

THREE YEARS AGO, at the end of summer, the little un-heard-of town called Spoonersville, was changed by the strange arrival of the orange Harvest Moon as well as... the DARK CIRCUS. Anyone who may have been foolish enough to pass by it would have been unaware that within in this carnival kingdom, there laid a twisted world of telepathic animals, freaks, living rides, and a mechanical gypsy. Anyone, that is, except for a *very* well-known trio of odd teenagers, who decided that same summer to take a ride up to the black oak tree next to the Old Bailey Lighthouse. These were the grounds where the abandoned circus seemed to be patiently waiting for the teens to arrive. A strong force pulled Daniel, Kyle, and Christy-Anne aka C.A. across those gates. Shortly after they entered, each received powers that matched their unique skills and personalities. Both the misshapen and the inhuman dwellers of that place bowed down to the three as the great masters, who controlled the Dark Circus: the MASTER MAGICIAN, the MASTER FREAK, and the MASTER TAMER. Eventually the kids managed to escape, and those three years moved along in a blink of an eye. It should have been over that night for the young masters. But it would seem fate, perhaps even Madame Fate, devised other plans for these three; not to mention the sudden second appearance of the same orange moon.

Tossing roughly in his sleep, with trickles of sweat sliding down the edges of his face, was sixteen-year-old Daniel Isaac Stephens. As gusts of wind pounded against his bedroom window, painful images went through his dreams. They were so intense and vivid that not only could he see different figures before him he could hear them as well. The first voice consisted of a horrible laugh, which he never forgot. It was the eerie chuckle of CHARLIE, the psychotic polka-dotted clown that nearly destroyed Daniel and his friends during their stay inside the circus. He remembered the last words they found in the unexplained time capsule that was buried next to the trio's own capsule at the oak tree. They haunted him every two months of the years that went by.

"HAVE YOUR VICTORY... WATCH THE NEXT FULL MOON... THE DARK CIRCUS WILL BE BACK... AND ILL SEE YOU SOON HAHAHAHAHAHAHAHAHAHAHAH AHA!"

The second voice was a faint yet foreign tongue. The one who spoke it bore the only face that Daniel couldn't see clearly. It constantly whispered to him over and over again, like a broken record,

"*Master... Master! Ahhhhhhhhhhhhha!*"

Further into the dream fire engulfed all around him. A crowd of millions stood on benches and in the isles. It was difficult to tell wither the frantic yelling and hollering could have been cheerful praise or screaming torture. Kyle and C.A. were in the dream too. In their forms as the Dark Circus Masters they stood before an evil creature in glittering purple robes. Both presented to this mysterious stranger as lambs on a sacrificial alter. Their bodies were bloody and burnt. The Master Magician's eyes became black hollows as he fell to his knees barely breathing at the site of the carnage performed on his friends.

Meanwhile, outside of his sleep, various objects shook off the shelves and the desk closest to Daniel's bed. The same demonic energy contained within the breeze that pressed against the window seeped into his room and caused minor cracks in the glass. Finally, the weight of it all burst the window wide open. The blast of wind hit Daniel hard enough to knock him down on his red- wood floor along with his pillows and blankets. Luckily for him, there were no major injuries. He slowly rose to his feet with the help of the grip he took on the only sheets left on the bed. The wind continued to blow in his face.

With his hands in front, Daniel pushed the air aside as he made his way over to close the window. The moment he touched the top of the glass a flash struck the back of his mind like a cannonball. He could see the robed dark figure of his dreams. This time the strange creature perched over him like a vulture. He or she demanded that the Magician make some crucial decision that may affect every single being on the planet.

"*It's time to choose, Heir of Desmond.*"

Desmond? Who was Desmond? he wondered to himself. After the flash stopped, the wind calmed down. It gently brushed against the tip of his peach lips. He couldn't explain it, but there was something familiar about that breeze... about everything he felt from the dream.

After the window was closed, he attempted to go back to sleep hoping that the nightmares would cease for the rest of the night. Aside from the grey clouds that passed the light of the full moon, there was another person watching from below. Whoever it was, appeared to know exactly what occurred in Daniel's room. He made himself invisible by sitting very still in an orange Dodge Challenger in the neighbors' driveway across from Daniel's house. Around the time the rest of the neighborhood slept and all seemed completely quiet, the stranger drove off hardly making a scratch on the pavement going down the road.

Chapter 2
Three New Faces

DANIEL SET OUT THE NEXT morning on his brand new black Road Runner moped. There were beautiful red stripes along the sides similar to the bike he once loved. Of course, to get it he worked overtime mowing lawns. He even sold some of his magic tricks online and to JOEY'S JOKE BOX SHOP.

His parents, the Stephens's, were a bit curious as to why their son would give up his need to perform sleight of hand. An amateur psychologist may have determined that perhaps the experience disturbed Daniel bad enough that he decided he didn't want anything more to do with magic. Everything else that reminded him of such a childish passion may have been locked away in his family attic for all he cared. He drove to 1753 Elliot Street...the home of the Spoonersville Giants... the elite institution of Morgan Hill High School.

On the outside, Morgan Hill resembled a traditional prep school. There was dull brown brick that made up the ten-foot walls, a bronze spit fountain in the middle of the curved driveway used by the buses held a sign with the school's name, and gorgeous trees that highlighted the surrounding sidewalks and bike paths on the outer edge of the zone line. "Gentlemen" were required to wear burgundy vests with the school crest of a giant with their own names underneath its feet, white short-sleeved-tuxedo shirts, tan slacks, and a yellow tie. While the "Ladies" wore the same vest, with tan skirts, white knee-high socks, and a white long-sleeved tuxedo shirts. Even though they all looked the same in their prestigious attire, as soon as Daniel arrived, the student body divided themselves amongst their own small cliques waiting for the bell.

Then again, there were those that kept to themselves, certain people who didn't think it at all unusual to play with small animals that came up to sit on their lap, people like Christy-Anne Rachel Curtis. Christy-Anne (or C.A. or the MASTER TAMER) grew into a beautiful young woman over the past three years. The cheerleaders offered C.A. a position on their squad many times, but at the same time, they would sneer at her or whisper disgusting things to one another about her. She sat below the chin of one of the two, large, marble lion statues on the front steps talking aloud to a squirrel. On a personal note, the statue seemed to have an uncanny resemblance to another lion she knew from the circus.

Waltzing over, Daniel couldn't help but eaves-drop during their conversation. He could hear her say to the squirrel in her lap,

"I brought you the no-salt peanuts this time. You really need to stop doing late-night scavenging through Mrs. Marcella's trash."

"And you need to stop talking to animals like they understand you," Daniel interrupted.

"Don't listen to him, Frederick."

"Frederick?"

"My little friend, here. You're certainly in a mood today."

"Sorry. I didn't get much sleep last night."

"I know."

"You know?"

"Frederick told me. He was on the branch outside your window last night. He said you fell off your bed."

"You're telling me a squirrel told you that?"

C.A. jumped down from the statue to get a little closer to Daniel to whisper, "You want to broadcast it?"

"If you want to hold a squirrel and talk to it on your own time, that's your thing, but you know you don't need to make up stories."

"I'm telling you Daniel..." C.A. covered Frederick's ears, "... I can hear this little fuzz-ball's thought. Now do I want to be able to hear his thoughts? No. And you know I consider myself a logical and rational person, but he has been jabbering to me for the last few days, ever since the full moon showed up."

"Oh great, now you're gonna bring the moon in this?"

"You know you don't need to..." C.A. started to create a scene by slightly raising her voice.

"C.A., C.A., I'm... I'm sorry. I'm not trying to make fun of you, okay. If you say you can talk to..."

"Frederick."

"Frederick, then I believe you. We okay now?"

They both took a breath then gave a little laugh before C.A. said, "Yeah, we're good."

"Good." Daniel leaned against the lion's statue where CA sat upon. He rubbed the bridge of his nose to stop the migraine he felt (in the past, his flashes, visions, or predictions were faint in the forms of migraines or headaches). The leaves of the trees around the school slightly shivered as if a breeze went by, although, no one else could feel it. C.A. immediately went into caring friend mode by sweetly asking,

"Bad dreams again?"

"Bad isn't the word for it. I'm starting to hear things now. I feel like I'm going crazy."

"We all go a little crazy sometimes..." a third voice came from the other side of the lion's statue. It belonged to none other than Kyle Ulysses Rogers (or the MASTER FREAK). He mimicked the line exactly like the character, Billy, from the movie, <u>Scream</u>. He sauntered around to place his head-on C.A.'s shoulders and decided to use his best Hannibal Lector voice

"... *Hello, Clarice...*"

"Grow up."

"Ah don't be such a girl, C.A."

"Freak, did I forget to tell you how much I hate you today?"

"I thought we rescheduled that for three o'clock."

"Humor is dead to me now." She rolled her eyes.

Not much changed for Kyle in the past three years. He was still into weird things as well as imitating other people. On the other hand, he seemed a bit more gothic appearance wise. Somehow, the school let it slide, but he could wear his long sleeves rolled up and on both of his arms, the Freak showed off his tattoos of two long Arabian swords. Across the swords were the names, Henry (on the right) and Clowey (on the left). They were the names of the midget man and the limbless young woman who aided him in his journey through the circus.

It must have been frustrating for Daniel. He wanted to let go of what happened; however, his friends just couldn't seem to do the same.

"Hey Houdini." He said to Daniel before surprising him with a headlock and kissing the top of his head.

The foul fumes' flowing from Kyle's armpits into Daniel's nose were enough to set off the atomic bomb. Then... he saw *them* walking up the stairs. There were three new faces at Morgan Hill, and it was clear that they were unlike anyone else Daniel ever noticed in Spoonersville before. There were two boys and one girl. Soon, C.A. and Kyle caught them in their sights to.

The girl wore a Japanese style haircut with different shades of blue and green highlights hidden within the blackness. Her eyes were thinly shaped and chestnut brown. Tightly clasped on her wrist was a twisted snake bracelet made of silver. Each snake possessed deep forest emerald eyes, which frightened Frederick and made him rattle in C.A.'s hands.

One of the boys looked like the offspring of a hippie or beatnik. His long, chestnut-shade hair wasn't just a part of his ponytail, but even more hair seemed to sprout behind his ears, which were slightly pointed. He wore black glasses, and his nails were jaggedly shaped and yellow.

The last of them obviously held the position of leader in their group. Not only did he give Daniel a brief psych-out glance that most athletes' give on the field, but as he walked the other two followed behind as obedient soldiers, who kept their eyes focused on the doors while marching up the stairs.

Compared to the other two, there didn't seem anything special about this guy, just the fact that he was a number ten on a scale for good-looking blonds. He continuously swirled these orange and black, plastic ping pong balls in one hand.

"Who are they?" Kyle asked in as though someone invaded his turf.

"I've never seen them before. Isn't it a little late in the quarter for new students?" C.A. inquired.

"I don't think they're new. Maybe we just didn't notice them before. Besides, who really wants to introduce themselves to seven hundred faces in one day." Daniel explained.

"I guess so," C.A. reassured herself.

The bell rang, causing a sea of students to find their way to their designated homerooms.

Chapter 3
Pick a Card, Cut a New One

SURELY IT WAS BY SOME "coincidence" that Daniel, Christy-Anne, and Kyle have always shared the same classes since they were little. Therefore, Mrs. Trisha Vadoma's history class would be no exception.

Mrs. Vadoma was another new addition to Morgan Hill High School. She was a foreign beauty with black raven hair that complemented her soft hazel eyes and the purple scarf that she kept around her neck. Although he couldn't explain it, Daniel would look at his new teacher and feel that she was connected to the one person he once trusted apart from his friends, the mechanical Madame Fate. According to the faculty notes in her record, Mrs. Vadoma never stayed in one place too long. The excuse she gave to the big shots in the main office for all the moving was family reasons.

One thing for sure was that she was no mouse. She took on a no-nonsense attitude that many teachers developed after being in a one school system for an extended period-of-time. She didn't even turn around when the second bell rang to settle down the students. The second she did address the class, the kids were in their seats with pencils in hand, attempting to avoid showing their teacher that look of worry that comes over when they don't have their homework ready to turn in.

"Alright, boys and girls, the first business of the day. As you all know, Morgan Hill is having a carnival as part of homecoming week for our seniors. It will be held October 31st from eight to eleven thirty at the Bailey Lighthouse grounds, despite my advice. So. I expect all of you to sign up for the volunteers list outside. We need people to run the games, food, and entertainment. Keep in mind that most of you need the extra credit, especially after the last test. Need I say more?"

The very mention of the lighthouse almost brought Daniel, Kyle, and C.A. to sit forward on the ends of their seats.

"...Next... due to the pipe burst in Mr. Up Chucks classroom we will be getting some stragglers for the next few months. So, without further ado, let's welcome Miss Diana Cameron Stewart (the girl with the snake bracelet), Mr. Andrew Ichabod Crew (the guy with the ponytail and shades), and Mr. Karl Richard Richmond Underberg (the blond) ..."

The new students strutted into the classroom with heads held high and snobbish, unimpressed looks on their faces.

"... Take your seats. Now I thought we'd start off the day with my favorite torture, open book review on the chapters related to the World War II."

The students responded in their own way with moans. Since no one wanted to get the ball rolling Mrs. Vadoma did what most students call the unthinkable. She decided to set her sights on those that were too distracted to see her come their way. Regularly, it was Kyle who would be put on the spot. Doodling on the side of his desk he waited to hear the teacher give the order to stand before the class and read... Therefore... the class was thrown for a loop when she asked Andrew.

"Mr. Crew, would you be so kind as to lend us your voice? And by the way, lose the glasses or die."

Andrew tilted his head in boredom. There was a moment that he shifted his eyes towards Karl for a response, but reluctantly, he did as she instructed. He stood at his desk and recited the text. The longer the passage the more irritated he became. He scratched the back of his ears (also out of boredom). The hair behind them shed beneath his nails and sprinkled on top of his desk. Some of the other students who witness the disgusting dandruff fall, covered up their laughter by clearing their throats or leaned away so they wouldn't catch any on their own books. The sound of their giggles compelled him to drop the shades to give them all a vicious, animal-like gaze. Only the presence of Karl behind him managed to temporarily keep Andrew in check.

C.A. couldn't take her eyes off Diana's bracelet, especially after seeing the way

Frederick reacted to it. It emulated a sinister mojo or aura around it. Diana slowly covered the bracelet with her hand than she coughed, looking straight at C.A. to let her know that Diana was strongly aware of what was on the Master Tamer's mind.

Daniel did his best to follow each word in the text verbatim. He glanced to his right side to see that Karl had done the same. Curiosity is a natural instinct when it came to checking out someone who may or may not have been the new kid on the block. Everything was fine for the first few minutes. Then, Daniel started to hear the sound of plastic rubbing together. Looking Karl's way, he noticed that the noise was from those ping pong balls. Over and over, in clock-wise rotation, they went.

The movement of the plastic was hard to ignore; even though Daniel pretended to care about the subject at hand. The more they circled, the quicker he became frustrated. He pressed the tip of his fingers to the temple of his head thinking that it would ease the pain of the horrible migraine that returned. Shortly, things began to get worse.

The sound was so irritating that it blocked out everything else. He felt as if he was underwater or that he experienced an out-of-body moment. His heart speed at a thousand beats per minute. His body remained still as something moved up through the back pocket of his slacks. Once the item freed itself, all Daniel could hear then was Karl dropping the plastic balls. The bounce briefly disrupted the class.

"Owe!" Karl snapped.

Daniel's hand fell flat to his desk as he started to breathe slowly but heavily

"No need to interrupt the class, Mr. Underberg."

Mrs. Vadoma moved to Karl's side ready to clean the long cut that formed across his wrist with wrapped bandages and alcohol. After she finished, she continued to pace back and forth observing the other students as if nothing happened. It did impose the question of how she knew to have those types bandages on stand-by for Karl so quickly. Some teachers may have kept a first aid kit in their desk, but for her to be prepared with clinical bandages appeared odd.

An inkling a free came across Daniel's face as he stared at what was right next to Karl's foot. Lying flat and unnoticed by anyone else was a card, a joker's wild card with a large red "X". Karl's blood was spotted on its edges. After class, Daniel picked it up. He didn't tell his friends about it; even when school let out. This was the Magician's triumph card, his great weapon of defense that contained a tiny fraction of his own power within itself.

Chapter 4
Down by the Riverside

KYLE WAS THE FIRST to be out of that educational prison as he called it. Unlike Daniel and C.A., who upgraded their modes of transportation (him with his moped; her with her new red and gold ten speed bike), Kyle stuck with his FREAK silver wheeled skateboard. Coming around the corner he performed a running start with his board, Tony Hawk style, when he bumped into Mr. Up-Chuck, who possessed a stomach big enough for sky divers to land on.

If there ever was a word to describe Mr. George Up-Chuck, then nothing could fit better than "annoying." A cheesy mustache, pudgy voice, and beady little eyes (magnified by round black spectacles) were all there was to him. Despite his sad pathetic features' Mr. Up-Chuck was not the type of person to be underestimated.

"Watch where you're going, Mr. Rogers!"

"What can I say, Up-Chuck. It's hard not to watch where *you're* going."

"You can't talk to me like that, young man. What's to stop me from walking you over to the Dean's office? That's the problem with you kids; you think you run the place. I swear. if it wasn't for the benefits..."

These ranting and threats from Mr. Up-Chuck happened every time he and Kyle crossed each other's paths. Kyle considered it a release to insult the man a little each day, but his attention changed once Andrew walked on the other side of the street. He changed his shirt from the school uniform to a black t-shirt with a wolf on the front. Then, he quickly rushed his way down a set of stairs next to the sidewalk.

"Look, Up Chuck; I got to go."

"This isn't over. Oh, no siree bob..." he said.

Kyle hurried around the corner out of ear range. Sadly, it didn't cease Up-Chuck's constant need to prattle on like a kindergartener the further he went.

"You'll pay for your insults soon enough, Master Freak!"

He raved on and on all the way to the janitor shed. Many people observed him going in there for the last three years; however, they never knew what he was up to in there. Even the custodian didn't know, since Up-Chuck made sure that he went in the shed at different times.

It looked as if Kyle made it his secret mission to catch up with Andrew. In truth, he had been curious since their minor encounter on the stairs. Andrew was headed for the river bank next to the edge of Pierce Park.

There were mixed emotions about entering such a place. Its dogma trees as well, as its pebble road by the river, could have been pulled out of a fairytale, and Kyle was certainly not into fairytales. So far, there was no sign of Andrew, only the river. The water appeared clear enough for a bear to scoop its paw in to pull out a fish. With nothing or no one around, he arrived at the conclusion that all this trouble to follow someone he didn't even know or care about seemed stupid. His friends were the ones to worry about things like that.

"Whatever. I'm out of here." Kyle said aloud to himself.

Soon he turned to leave. The wind blew against Kyle's ears, causing them to twitch and stop for a second. He brushed it off then tried to leave again... but the wind blew across once more. This time, it spoke in whispers to him.

"*Master Freak.... Master... Freak....*"

It went on, saying this with each slow step away from the river. At the same time, Andrew patiently used the trees around to hide as he watched Kyle. He even removed his sun glasses to amplify the danger. As he reached midway to exit the park, Kyle's instincts forced him to spin around to face the voice, which called out for him. That's when he saw that he wasn't exactly in Kansas anymore. His mind created a magnificent hallucination. The trees that were once vibrant with color transformed into something black as if they were badly burned in fire. Going pass them on his way to the river Kyle could see shadows everywhere. He looked down near his feet and noticed this *thing* sniffing about the ground searching frantically with its hands for something to eat. It was the cannibal boy from the Dark Circus. The same boy who bore a collar around his neck, blood from his mouth, and ripped clothes. He smiled at Kyle with a demon's' glee. Then, he went further down the path.

Kyle approached the river once again as well as each of the trees. By the second time there were other shadows of his old circus friends popping out from behind the barks and branches.

The bird woman, with the ravens beak and ostrich legs in her hot pink glitter dress, perched herself high on a branch possibly smiling (but it was difficult to tell); the fat man lifted weights in his tight cheetah spotted leotard, while his brother, the strong man, in the same leotard, repeatedly groomed the fine lines of his barbershop mustache; the four-legged girl in the emerald dress played with a broken marionette puppet; the conjoined twin brothers in their purple plaid suits were bowing to Kyle like noble men; and lastly, Clowey waited at the end of the path by the water for her master. Even holding the switch blade in her mouth, she still maintained a warm, innocent smile. The only one missing was Henry, the midget man in the suit.

She did her best to move aside (for someone with neither legs or arms to do so). Kyle dropped his skateboard to bend down on his knees into see in the water. Upon the blurred ripples of his reflection, his teeth were sharp and jagged. His eyes were black, which matched his spiked hair. He touched his face, not realizing that his fingernails changed into his former silver talons. What happened next was not an intentional part of the illusion from which he suffered.

Andrew stealthily surfaced from the trees towards Kyle in an animal sprint on all fours. His eyes glowed bright gold... his hair out and flowing in sync with the beat of his speed. He jumped high in the air prepared to tackle down the enemy. That is, until Henry finally emerged as a part of Kyle's reflection. He smiled and told Kyle in a frantic tone

"Behind you, master!!!" Henry warned him.

Kyle quickly reacted in time to catch Andrew on his chest. The two of them rolled around until they pushed one another a part into their own neutral corners. There were deep impressions of the Freak's nails displayed in Andrew's neck. Kyle's fingernails and the side of his mouth were splattered with small traces of his opponent's blood. He grossly licked the blood off then rubbed underneath his nose.

The park transformed back to its normal beauty. Andrew quickly put his shades on and Kyle whipped his nails along his pants.

"What the hell's your problem?" Kyle demanded.

"You're the one who was stalking me!"

"Oh yeah? Good stalkers don't get jumped on."

"Depends on the prey." Andrew glared beneath his glasses.

"Tell me about it." Kyle agreed, unaware that his talons returned to being ugly fingernails.

"What do you want, anyway?"

"Nothing. It's just, no one ever comes over here."

"What are you, the park ranger?"

"Actually, I'm the town Freak; haven't you heard?"

Andrew took a small pause to make it seem as if he hardly had a clue; when in fact as Kyle and the other young masters would learn, this Spoonersville new comer knew more than he let on about the *real* world from where they came.

Kyle made his way back to the river. Andrew followed at a safe distance. This time, when he decided to kneel-down to the water, he scooped a good portion of the tiny waves to splash his face and clean his nails. There was a moment, as he continued to dip his hands, when he thought he would see Henry's face in the ripples. But nothing... for the moment at least. Andrew left his belongings by one of the trees close to the right side of Kyle. Once he collected them, he saw the stairs and began to walk towards them. The Freak knew he wouldn't be surprised a second time by this guy so he didn't even bother to look behind. The shadows of his Dark Circus freaks still lingered around him as a sign of protection for their master. Both the strong man as well as the bird woman (who placed her head against the back of his shoulder ready to strike with her beak) escorted him towards the exit.

The boys were back at the top near the street. Kyle wore a reluctant expression that some people were known to wear before they apologizing to another. Since he wasn't really an apologetic type of guy, doing such a thing was not ideal; However, he swallowed his pride and ran up the stairs.

"Hey. Hey. Hey, stop..."

Andrew stopped as he bounced his head sideways back at Kyle

"Look, I'm sorry about what happened back there. Where did you learn how to fight like that anyway?"

"What are you, a reporter?"

"Just one of those people who can't seem to mind their own business."

Andrew hesitated a couple minutes then he responded with a half-smile to demonstrate a truce. They both laughed a little.

"Uh, I got a Wii System at home. My best game is Just Dance. I have a mad record."

"Disturbing... I'm Kyle." He officially introduced himself with a fist bump jester.

"Andrew. I remember you from class. By the way, where did *you* learn how to fight?"

"About ten minutes ago, when you pulled one of your dance moves on me."

"Hey, let's get something straight, okay? You were the one playing stalker. I got to admit, though, that was a good defense move. It was very wax on wax off."

"You making fun of me?"

"A little bit. Maybe you shouldn't make it so easy with the way you dress."

At last, the Freak discovered someone else with the same peculiar sense of humor.

"Don't even get started with that, caveman dude. How long have you been around?" Kyle asked.

"Don't hate the shag, man; the ladies love it."

"Keep telling yourself that; you may start to believe that crap."

"Hahaha. I like your style, Freak. It's just too bad I couldn't rig the pipes to go off sooner so we could've had a chat like this earlier."

"Shut the front door ..." Kyle replied slightly surprised "... You made the pipes go off?"

"Ah, Up-Chuck had it coming. The guy's a loser anyway."

"Tell me about it (**Kyle started to imitate Mr. Up Chuck's voice**): *YOU CAN'T TALK TO ME LIKE THAT* yadda yadda yadda."

"What was that?"

"What? Oh, it's a thing I do. Ask anybody they'll tell you. It is a small town after all."

"Huh? You want to come over and play on Wii? I can show you more of my moves if you want."

"As long as we don't spring into a chorus of Kumbaya." Kyle said.

"You have to take me out to dinner first for that."

Off they went. It was such a mood changer. One minute, they're fighting the next second, they're way to see who can do the best conga.

Chapter 5
A Charmer in the Greenhouse

CHRISTY-ANNE WENT HOME eagerly not only because she thought that school was a prison like Kyle did, but also to get away from all the bad mojo that emulated from Diana's bracelet. She searched for Frederick after school with no luck. Then again, she figured it wouldn't be hard for him to find his way to her house. It was the only one on *Cage House Lane* with a greenhouse and a barnyard in the back.

Inside the tempered glass walls of that greenhouse C.A. took great care of the animals. Since her adventure at the Dark Circus three years ago, they each seemed to be more affectionate with her, including the snakes... who she visited first. Every day after school since she was five, she gained the task of making sure not only to feed them, but to make sure to clean up their dead skin, and collect samples of venom for her father's analysis. She didn't even have to lift them out of their metal tub with a rod like her father. She placed her arm deep in and one at a time they'd wrap around her. A red corn snake named Jeffery, who was the baby compared to the rest, appeared the most playful. He always snuck out when CA wasn't looking to try to bother the other animals. But that day was different.

Just as Christy-Anne scrapped a sample from Petunia, their viper, and whispered to her

"Very good, Petunia. That wasn't so bad, was it?"

Jeffery slithered to the door. He could sense someone there, which most young snakes such as himself could do so because of a defense mechanism. Part of the perks of being the Master Tamer was that if the snake could sense it, so could C.A. That same negative energy softly pushed open the door and picked up Jeffery like a professional charmer.

"Well, hello there. Aren't you beautiful," she said. C.A walked towards the two of them.

"You must be Christy-Anne. We had class together this morning."

"Yeah, I remember. Listen, I'm sorry for staring at your uh..."

"Bracelet? That's okay. A lot of people do."

"How did you know where I lived?"

"Uh..." she hesitated to come up with a lie, "...the school yellow book. It lists everyone's address and phone number."

"Oh, right. What are you doing here?"

"The carnival's next week. You and I are signed up for being in-charge of the food. Mrs. Vadoma asked me to stop by, so we can plan on what to get so the school can deduct it from the budget."

"My name was on there, today?"

"Is there a problem?"

"No, not at all. I wasn't going to sign up until tomorrow, but I guess..."

"You know, you got some nice reptiles here, especially this cutie. He's such a flirt. Then again, most males are. You know what I mean?"

"Thank you."

"Of course, you know that thirty percent of the world's population is still afraid of snakes."

"And only twenty percent realize that certain venom isn't as fast to kill as regular venom is."

"I'm impressed."

Another stranger from class entered the greenhouse...Karl.

"Diana, you in here?" asked Karl.

"Yes, back here!" She yelled back.

"Hey, how's it going? I'm Karl."

He reached out to shake CA's other hand since she still held onto Petunia. Petunia made small hissing sounds as if she was going into a defensive mode. Diana gazed at her viciously and Petunia went back to being quiet.

"Christy-Anne. Everybody calls me C.A. I remember you from class, too."

"Here I thought that Diana was the only one with a whole menagerie at her house."

"I know, I was just telling her she had a good selection," Diana explained while kissing and caressing Jeffery.

"Hope it's alright if I stay I'm Diana's ride."

"You drive?"

"A dodge challenger. My dad got it for me from the junkyard. I just finished getting it all together, course it took a lot of... magic."

"Ha, it's funny... Daniel would know more about magic than me. He's a magician... well, I mean... he practices that sort of thing. Or rather, he used to." CA laughed, trying to cover up her worry for what she almost let slip about the circus.

Right away, she placed Petunia back in the tub and went with Diana to make their list of all the food and supplies they would need for the carnival. As the ladies worked Karl perched himself on top one of the lab tables. He reached into his pocket to take out the same plastic ping pong balls he used at school. Instead of swirling them in his hand like before he began to juggle them high in the air. He was so good that he could look past them to keep his focus on the girls. No matter how fast they were moving he didn't have to try hard to make sure they landed in his hands. It was like a magnetic attraction.

The scratch on his wrist started to open, again. To Karl, the wound felt numb to the pain.

Chapter 6
Follow the Polka Dots

THE FULL MOON STAYED in the sky for the rest of the week and Daniel continued to struggle with his dreams. All the images overlapped, and the voices he heard in his previous dreams constantly changed. There was one that clearly spoke to him

"You were right not to trust me... this is only the beginning Heir of Desmond... only the beginning..."

Daniel jumped from his bed. His chest tight he grasped it to gain his breath again.

What did all this mean? What possible connection did he have with this Desmond? Nothing made sense, anymore. Perhaps there may have been some answers in a certain little box with the last of his old magic tricks. As soon as the Saturday morning came Daniel made his way to see Joey at Spoonersville's own Joke Box Shop.

The JOKE BOX: COMPENDIUM of GUARANTEED PRANKS & HUMOR was an establishment introduced to Daniel through his brother, Tommy, who retired from the game of pulling a fast one on the older sibling. Although the day went by slowly Joey was one of those "eccentric" people who could always find ways to keep themselves occupied. Daniel inhaled a deep breath before going inside. He convinced himself that once they were gone, he would never have to look at those tricks, again. Then the young magician found a surprise as he could see ahead of him, waiting for Joey at the counter to pass by on his moving ladder, was Mr. Up-Chuck.

He walked up beside him. Mr. Up-Chuck turned his head, giving off a small fearful shiver towards Daniel.

"Hey, Mr. Up-Chuck. How are you?"

"Fine, fine, I'm just fine. And whoever has told you otherwise is lying."

"Okay. Just asking."

Up-Chuck began to sweat. His knees were practically shaking and he did a poor job at trying to hide his face. If Daniel cared, he would have noticed right away that Up-Chuck was hiding something. Suddenly, Joey zipped around with the item that Up-Chuck wanted to purchase.

"Here, we are Upster. That'll be $12.54." Joey said.

He wasted no time in paying cash in-order to get out the door at the speed of light. He was in such a rush to leave that he forgot a piece of cloth on the counter. It looked like a handkerchief. The colors and design of the piece were very familiar to Daniel. It was yellow with black polka dots. He didn't chase after Up-Chuck; even though the cloth further fueled the Master Magician's curiosity.

"What a very strange dude." laughed Joey.

"Does he always come in here?"

"At least three times a year. So, what can I do for you, Danny boy?"

"Do you remember the shoe box I gave you a while back? There was a deck of cards inside and a paperback handbook."

"Oh, yeah good stuff. Actually, someone bought the box two weeks ago, A lady I think. Do you want to look at some of my new stock?"

"A lady? What did she look like?"

"Come on, Danny boy; don't they all look the same."

"What would she want with an old shoe box?"

"Hey, don't ask, don't tell; that's my policy."

"You don't have a policy Joey."

"Good point."

"That's okay, anyway. I'll see you later." He said to Joey

Daniel left the shop annoyed. That box was the key that could possibly help him to understand what was happening with the dreams and maybe even with the new guy, Karl. He couldn't get over the way he looked at him going up the school stairs. It was a challenge. One thing he did leave with was the polka dotted handkerchief. He put it in the back of his pocket next to the wildcard he kept from class.

The original plan was to return it next week to Mr. Up-Chuck. On his way, home a sudden flash struck Daniel hard in the back of his head as he was driving along on his moped coming up past Elliot Street. The pain made him wobble and lose his balance. He fell next to a bench that was located in the far closed area of Morgan Hill.

In each flash, Daniel saw Charlie, but only his smile. Then once the flash stopped, he had seen Up-Chuck anxiously scratching the lock on the janitor shed. He noticed that after he could open the shed, Up-Check bore more black polka dots, except that they were visible on his yellow socks. Daniel was determined to cease his investigation for the day, and to go home to rest before meeting his friends at eight.

Behind closed doors, in the most unsuspecting of places, was Mr. Up-Chuck. He wiped the dust that was on the only window in the shed to ensure that no one was watching. As soon as the coast was clear, he pulled the cord of the over-head lamp attached to the ceiling to help him find his way through a long, red, velvet curtain. The light revealed that what Mr. Up-Check had entered was some sort of shrine. In the center leaning against the back was a large cracked mirror surrounded by black and red candles. A nineteenth-century gramophone situated by the exit played broken music. Up-Chuck commenced to speak to the mirror in a giddy, fan-type manner,

"Master... I'm here."

"PATIENCE, MY SERVANT, FOR YOU HAVE DONE WELL..." that horrible rhyming,

"... THE TIME IS UPON US TO BREAK THIS SPELL...

HAHAHAHAHAHAHA."

"Master, I have what you asked me to get, but I still don't understand why we have to..."

"SILENCE, YOU PUDGY, LITTLE TROLL! NEVER FORGET THAT I AM IN CONTROL! NOW, SHOW ME THE CAPE THAT WILL ENSURE MY ESCAPE."

Up-Chuck laid the item flat on the floor and placed some of the candles on its edges to make sure it didn't wrinkle.

"It is ready master."

"EXCELLENT."

Charlie's hand moved through the mirror, like jelly, to reach for the cape. However, it didn't make it all the way. The power that was maintaining him on the other side wouldn't let him pass through just yet.

"DRAT! I FORGOT ABOUT THAT... HAHAHA... OH WELL, ALL GOOD THINGS COME TO THOSE WHO WAIT. IS EVERYTHING PREPARED FOR TONIGHT AT EIGHT?"

"Yes, master."

"GOOD, MY SERVANT. I COMMAND YOU TO GO. LET'S GIVE SPOONERSVILLE A FRIGHTFUL SHOW. AND SHOULD THE GYPSY BE THERE TO ATTEND... LET'S PLAN OUT HER HORRIBLE DISMAL END,"

Charlie vanished within the mirror like smoke; while his loyal lackey was off to do his as commanded. Things were becoming dangerous.

Chapter 7
Trouble at the Lighthouse

EIGHT O'CLOCK WENT by fast. Daniel intended to meet up with Kyle and C.A. at the local hangout in town... Although, going would prove to be a more difficult task than anticipated.

It was the week of Halloween. Usually, there were a few teenagers from school that happened to pop up at the local café, The Cup, or took up space on the sidewalk. Every citizen in Spoonersville constantly maneuvered in and out of stores for costumes and supplies. Traditionally, being in such a small town, people would appear just as busy for any other holiday such as Christmas, Easter, and Valentine's Day; Not to mention the fact that this was also the week of the big homecoming game: The Morgan Hill Giants versus the Lansbury Academy Hawks. The game ended 20-10... a great confidence booster for the town since it was the tenth time in a row they'd beaten the Hawks.

As Daniel rode in on his moped, both sides of the street were filled with students passing out tickets to promote the anticipated carnival. "*It's almost funny...*" he thought briefly to himself, "*...that so many people could get excited about something so cheesy.*" On the other hand, Daniel could understand their excitement once the sound of a violin and tambourine playing by the ice cream shop may also have peaked the people's interest.

A huge crowd surrounded the musicians. Inside the circle of bodies, people became hypnotized by the echo of a woman's voice singing and her angelic yet wild dancing. Once Daniel found his way to the front of the commotion, he was in total awe at the sight of the woman dancing and singing so beautifully. It was none other than Mrs. Vadoma. Her raven shade hair he'd seen tightly pulled back in class flowed out smoothly. Instead of her usual conservative ensemble, she wore a jean jacket adorned with bedazzle jewels that covered a purple and green dress like a gypsy outfit that may be seen at a renaissance fair. People clapped with a steady beat as she performed her routine.

"Come, Sweet children
Come with me
To a land of fear and fantasy
Come, Sweet Children
You can stay, and we can play all day
But
Beware, Sweet Children
Danger's near
Your dreams will never be quite clear
Still the land is magic, dark, and free
So, Sweet
Children, will you come with me.........."

The crowd continued to give her great applause. She took her bows then lowered her head down enough so that she could quickly flip her hair back and run her fingers through it. A gorgeous smile framed her face. The students were in complete surprise about how cool their teacher was compared to the stiff-necked Nazi that confronted them every weekday morning. Then, she made an announcement.

"Thank you, everyone. Please come with me, as well as the rest of the student body, to our first Morgan Hill High School Carnival. There will be food and *this* type of entertainment. So please, let's get the week rolling. Thank you, again."

She took another bow. As soon as the crowd dispersed to go on with their shopping sprees or whatever, Daniel could see that to the far right of him, Kyle and CA stood; they were already eating ice cream with Karl, Diana, and Andrew. The girls were the only ones eating the ice cream. Karl continued to show off his impressive juggling. Andrew horsed around with Kyle by teaching him some of his fight movements.

Even though, Daniel motioned over to them in a calm mood, secretly he felt an annoying aggravation in the pit of his stomach. Karl was the first to acknowledge him.

"Hey, glad you could make it..." Karl began, "...Daniel, right? Or is it Houdini?"

"Daniel's fine. I see you guys have gotten cozy."

"Oh yeah, your friends are great. Listen, I'm sorry if we gave you the wrong impression on the stairs at school."

"Don't worry about it, man."

Then CA sauntered by with Diana sticking ever by her side.

"Hey, what's wrong? You look mad or something."

"No, I'm not mad. Not at all."

Kyle and Andrew were the next ones to come over. The way Kyle praised his new friend almost seemed more frightening than Kyle himself.

"Dude! Never try to beat this man at Call of Duty; his system is rocking. I mean, Andrew here's got an original SEGA Genesis hooked up to play station 2 and 3. He's got a 5.1 surround sound system connected to a new LCD TV. He's totally into punk. He likes Death Dogs and Howling Meany's. He is sick."

"Sounds like someone needs a cold shower." Daniel advised, "How's your scratch?" Daniel asked Karl.

"I don't think I'll be signing my will any time soon. Why did you take the card?"

"Card?"

"The one you picked up after class. The one that had my blood on it. Unless you're a vampire and you like to lick blood off the edges of things."

The gang laughed. Kyle coughed into his hand since the others didn't know that he really did lick blood off his own fingers earlier in the park during his confrontation with Andrew.

"The card just reminded me of something." Daniel shrugged his shoulders

"Well, I was just curious. Say, did you guys want to hang out with us, tomorrow?"

Karl's manner made Daniel more suspicious. In fact, as he approached, the young magician's eyes started to sting. He was forced to blink his lids roughly, because he didn't want the others to think he was weeping. This was the start of one of his visions. It appeared to him as constant flashes of orange light, which revealed Karl as two people. There was the normal Karl before him... then a version of Karl as a figure whose skin completely changed and was covered in orange and black checker patterns. On top of his head he wore an orange jesters hat and diamond imprinted vest. Despite seeing this moving vision, Daniel didn't want to cause a scene in front of his friends or the rest of the town.

"I'm up for it. How about you, Freak?" C.A. responded with eyes slightly wide with joy.

"You know I'm there," Kyle said giving Andrew one of those guy handshakes.

"What about you, Daniel?" Diana's said with her eyes focused in a flirting manner.

Christy-Anne was slightly jealous; although she would never admit it.

Daniel tried to give his answer to Karl, but the pain that attacked him pricked the back of his mind, which made it hard to concentrate. His vision slowly turned groggy and he could see the words across Diana, Andrew, and Karl's faces: "*Don't...Enemy.... Beware young master... Beware.*" Regardless of the signs the hallucination warned him of, the only reply Daniel could utter,

"Sure, why not. So, you guys ready to go do that thing..." Daniel looked at his friends.

"What thing?" Kyle asked.

"What are you talking about?" C.A. joined in Kyle's confusion.

"Ah, you know... that thing... for the... you know the thing." Daniel's mumbling worked to get the other two to follow him. "We'll see you, tomorrow, Karl, Andrew, and uh..."

"Diana. My name's Diana."

"Diana, right."

Daniel quickly guided his friends in the direction away from the ice cream shop. Kyle and C.A. trotted along close by their fearless leader.

"Let's go," Karl ordered his posse

They traveled down an alley to disappear into the rest of the night. As they left, Andrew continuously scratched while looking at the full moon, which seemed to last longer than most moons do in a month. Diana whispered sweetly to her bracelet as its eyes glowed, "Patience, baby." Karl, their ring leader, smiled very snobbishly. Obviously... they were all up to no good.

"Houdini, what thing were you talking about?"

"Yeah, why'd we have to leave...?"

"I just got a bad feeling from those three."

Only moments after Daniel explained his behavior, trouble started to occur at the Old Bailey Lighthouse. Everyone on the street nearly contracted whip-lash when they had heard a loud BOOM in the direction of the Lighthouse. They all took a gasp of breath as they witnessed it crumble, and the shock of another BOOM finally brought the historic landmark down to the ground. Soon, people were running up the hill to the lighthouse, which blocked the ambulance, fire trucks, and local law enforcement from entering the perimeter.

It had been a long time since the young masters returned up that winding road of the hill. Perhaps Daniel and his friends should have been worried or scared even, that the whole town might see traces left behind by the Dark Circus (the gold and black dust from the flyers that enticed them to walk inside the grounds). Upon arrival, the trio seemed more troubled about the state of the oak tree and their sacred time capsule buried beneath its' roots.

The police did their best to hold the citizens back behind the tape. The kids could see that the extent of the destruction to the lighthouse destroyed along with the damage to the tree, which was pulled out of its roots. Below, protruding from the dirt, was the time capsule. A closer look indicated that it wasn't the same capsule that they always had; it was the second capsule the teens discovered after abruptly leaving the circus (the one with Charlie's message). After that summer, they threw the old one away and combined what was in it with the new one.

Daniel nodded his head as a signal for Kyle to sneak over and grab the capsule. He moved when he thought the officers weren't looking. He crouched to the ground crawling like a spider. The moment that he reached for the box one of the police went to approach Kyle.

"Hey kid, you can't cross the line." He said.

Squeaking behind C.A. was Frederick. He scratched her ankle to get her attention. They engaged in each other's eyes, allowing her to speak to him through her mind. She instructed him to distract the officer so that the Freak could take the capsule. Frederick obeyed with all speeds by rushing up his leg then scurried all over his entire body. The officer's' hands flew everywhere. It was very amusing. The officer's partner came over to get Frederick off, but they couldn't help laughing. Kyle grabbed the box and reappeared by Daniel, who intensely observed the scene, which was not only the lighthouse, but also the gate across from it.

More and more flashes from the past came to Daniel through the night. Shaking his head and rubbing his eyes was the only thing to help ease them momentarily. By the end of the tape, to his opposite side, Daniel could see Mr. Up- Chuck. He smiled an ugly smile looking at the fall of one of the town's landmarks. Green slime dripped from his mouth, but Up-Chuck wiped it with his inner sleeve colored yellow with black polka dots... always with the polka dots. The minute that Up- Chuck spotted Daniel watching him, he quit grinning like an idiot and left the area.

Finally, the rest of the town commenced to leave down the hill. But before Daniel followed the bunch he noticed as he turned his neck that the remaining officers were holding long red and black balloons used to make animals for children. Daniel could also hear them say that each one was filled with explosive chemicals attached to a small fuse.

Chapter 8
Madame...Vadoma?

ALONG WITH THE REST of the town, C.A. and Kyle were already down the road, headed for home. They were still thinking about the lighthouse and the capsule. However, what Christy-Anne became preoccupied about how strange Daniel was acting. She figured it couldn't all be from his bad dreams. She had an inkling of a feeling that there may have been some truth in what he was saying about having a bad feeling about their new friends, given the way Diana looked at him, and given her strange bracelet.

Daniel hung back, taking his time to return to his moped. He was ready to start it, up until Mrs. Vadoma stepped out of thin air.

"Come with me."

"You almost gave me a heart attack!" He jumped.

"Come with me, now. There's something you have to see."

"Look, Mrs. Vadoma I'm just trying to go home. The show you put on was great, by the way. I really liked the kicks and the song."

Daniel turned the key, but the engine lacked any sense of life.

"Well, that's why I'm here for your amusement. Of course, Mr. Stephens, it would be hard for you to get anywhere without this."

Mrs. Vadoma twirled between the fingers of her hand to show a small tube that was soiled from motor oil. Daniel's eyes rapidly searched to see that not only was he on empty, but the small part connected with the engine and the gas tank had gone.

"I have gas and what you need to fix your ride in two minutes. But first, you have to come with me."

She pranced away (down the alley that Karl and his friends had gone into) whistling the song she had sung. He didn't want to go, but given the fact that his life seemed to be one big pin ball machine that had a weird way of hitting him up and down away from the hole, Daniel figured why not further complicate his life.

Daniel jogged after Mrs. Vadoma so he could hurry to see what she wanted to show him. He assumed the alley he entered stood abandoned (just as he assumed three years ago, that the lot across from the fallen lighthouse was empty). The violin, from earlier in the main-street, played a faster livelier tune. Further down the alley, there burned a bonfire and there were sounds of more people reselling within such a condensed area.

All of them appeared to be speaking amongst themselves in their native family tongue of old world Russia or something. Rounding the corner, Daniel saw Mrs. Vadoma leading him into a small gypsy caravan. Children danced around the fire. An old man, whose was clearly the eldest gypsy and contained their people's wisdom in his deep wrinkles, sat in his favorite green and white lawn chair, smoking from an Indian smoke pipe. The few men present were busy drinking and moving boxes and luggage in the station wagons, Volkswagens, and trucks. The women were talking amongst themselves, fearful at the sight of whom Vadoma had brought into their sacred ground.

She took Daniel inside a blue trailer plastered with stars across its sides. Above the broken screen door, was a sign that read **MADAME VADOMA**. All the pieces of furniture including the couch, floors, windows, and table with the crystal ball, were covered in different colored scarves. An old woman wearing a hot pink scarf and a night-gown that could have been robbed from the local asylum was happily embroidering a patch on a black robe. She sat on the couch beneath a poster of imprinted with the image of the MARVELOUS MADAME FATE. Daniel's mouth dropped as he noted this feeble old woman shared the same features as the poster.

"Go ahead..." Mrs. Vadoma said, "...Have a seat." She then started to speak to the old woman in the language the others used outside. Roughly, translated she said,

"Momma, where is the box you bought from the store?"

"Why?" she responded still happily in her own world.

"It's for the boy, momma. The one you had the vision about."

The old woman stopped her work the minute she heard the word vision. She began to mumble and rose from the couch with arms wide out, but Mrs. Vadoma manage to prevent her mother from continuing.

"Momma..." she said, "... the box?"

"Oh, yes."

The old woman wandered off in the back of the trailer, hopefully to find the object her daughter asked for. Even though his eyebrows were raised for most of the visit in his teacher's home, Daniel knew that things would only get freakier, so he advocated to stay in a semi-sane and positive mind-frame.

"Are you a fortuneteller?" he casually asked.

"On the weekends, the best and brightest of Spoonersville come to see me or my mother for love advice. You know, palm reading, that sort of thing."

The old woman came back ever smiling with box in hand. Daniel immediately recognized that it was the box in which he stuffed his main magic tricks (the one that he sold to Joey at the Joke Box.). Ms. Vadoma gently took the object from her mother. She yelled outside to a little girl carrying a large book.

"Sit at the table," Vadoma commanded in her teaching tone.

As soon as Daniel did what she asked, he was pulled suddenly across the table by the old woman. At first, he panicked because this crazed senior citizen had a mean grip. Then Mrs. Vadoma put her hands on his shoulders, acting as his comfort. She whispered to him,

"It's alright, Master Magician. It's alright."

She reached, with one hand, into the box to pull out Daniel's old set of magic cards. She laid them on the center of the table, while her mother began to chant in deep meditation with her eyes closed. Soon, her mouth opened with fire blazing wildly inside. It reminded him of his dreams. His mind was sent out of his body, like a kite, and all around him the cards from the deck circled him and the two women with great speed.

Daniel's spirit became frozen as he watched chaos happen around him. Time no longer moved, not even Mrs. Vadoma anymore. Just silence was the only thing the Magician could interact with (which wasn't easy with the old woman's hands still upon him). Thankfully, he was not alone in the world that he was sucked into by this magic. Next to him appeared Madame Fate. She lifted her mechanical left hand in a motion like a clock, and like magnets, the X card from Daniel's pocket flew to it, as well as the polka dotted cloth. With her eyes, glowing bright, she began to speak

"*The clown has convinced the devils mistress of your ignorance, Magician. Trust no new faces nor let your comrades fall to the charms of his minions. For the other masters' will be punished and tested as well. The audience of both worlds shall be expecting the heir of Desmond the MYSTIC to appear. He will demand satisfaction for the law which has been tainted... I will be with you... young master...*"

In a snap, Daniel returned to his body, the trailer, Mrs. Vadoma, and her screwball mother. He suffered a mild loss of hearing, and his vision was a little blurred.

"Daniel. Daniel. What did you see?" Mrs. Vadoma still held onto his shoulders. Now she spoke to him a like a regular adult figure, but there was also a detection of anxiety in her voice as she continued to question him. "Did you see her? What did she say?"

He brushed her off, stared at her, then ran out the door. He didn't even bother to grab the gas can that was promised to him in exchange for going with her on a trip to psycho-vile. She wanted to chase after him, but he was clear gone by the time she reached the street.

She walked back unaware that above one of the buildings that made up the alley was Andrew. His shades were off along with his shoes, revealing his hairy feet with toe nails that were longer than his fingernails. His hair, out of the pony-tail, flowed softly in the wind of the night. When he'd seen all that he needed to, he left to inform his friends.

The whole thing was crazier than the hair on Albert Einstein's head. Mystery piling on top of mystery, and the danger, which obviously involved something other than

Charlie, was surfacing. It was clear that Spoonersville hadn't seen anything, yet.

Chapter 9

The Legend of the MYSTIC Desmond

DURING THE DAY, October 30th, the eve of the carnival, Daniel sat on the steps, waiting to have lunch with his friends. Truthfully, he was glad that they were running late in meeting him. He didn't even know if he could tell them what had happened. Kyle maybe, but Christy-Anne not so much.

As soon as Kyle and C.A. arrived, Daniel could see that they brought their new friends along. That is, except for Andrew. He was marked down as absent for the day. The pit of his stomach and the ordeal he experienced the night before increased Daniel's resistance to Karl.

"What kept you guys?" Daniel asked with a frustrated expression

"Oh, that was my fault..." Karl responded, "... I was just showing off a few tricks by my car. You want to see?"

"I'll take a raincheck."

Christy-Anne sat to the right of him; while Diana sat to the left. Both girls were comforting him with their hands on his arms.

"You alright?" C.A. asked.

"You know me, C.A., I'm just the life of the party."

"Are you sure there's nothing we can do for you." Diana tilted her head, sweetly catching C.A.'s jealous glance.

He replied with a smile and nod.

"So, where's your buddy Andrew?"

"Sick. We're going by his house after school to see if he's still up for going to the carnival. Are you guys going?" Karl answered back like a whip.

"The whole thing sounds lame..." Kyle said, "...but if C.A. and Daniel are going more than likely I'll be there."

"Yeah, as if we control your life, Freak." C.A. scoffed.

"Your life, Freak (he imitated her). You know, I think I'm gonna have to go to the school shrink for that insult, C.A." Kyle said rolling his eyes.

Just when it seemed like this would turn into a bigger argument than need be. Daniel rose from the stairs.

"I'll catch you guys later." He moaned, leaving everyone with concerning looks.

"Way to go, Freak." C.A. said.

"Whatever," Kyle said walking inside the moment the bell rang.

C.A. went in with Karl and Diana, who looked at one another with satisfying glee.

It's not easy when a young man loses his mode of transportation. He becomes attached to it as if it's a member of the family. At the end of the day, Daniel presumed that he would be trotting his way home by foot since he left his moped back at the alley. But, he nearly vapored up the second he saw that it was right in front of the school. He ran to it and kissed every inch. The whole scene was disgusting. He wasted no time in hoping onto the seat to take off. Then showing up out of nowhere once more, dressed in her normal school attire, appeared Mrs. Vadoma in the street to block his direction. Daniel couldn't see any way of maneuvering around her.

"We need to talk."

"No offense, Mrs. Vadoma, but I think I've had enough weirdness for one day. Besides, I have to go pick out my costume for the carnival."

"Ah come on now, Mr. Stephens. Last night shouldn't have been so bad for you, especially when you consider everything you and the other masters had to do to defeat Charlie."

Daniel held his breath for five seconds, then he claimed denial.

"Sorry. I don't know what you're talking about."

"Yes, you do, Daniel. Or should I say the Heir of Desmond?"

Again, he held his breath and tried to act as if he was completely clueless.

"Your dreams only have part of the answer. There are things that must be done tomorrow." She explained.

A dusty 1970's station wagon drove alongside them. It was the same station wagon that Daniel saw in the alley. At the wheel sat the old man, whom Daniel recalled sitting in the green and white lawn chair smoking a pipe. In the passenger seat was the little girl, who carried the sacred book to Mrs. Vadoma after she called for her. Her little hands held onto it once more.

Mrs. Vadoma walked over to the car to take the book to give to Daniel.

"Look inside; you might learn something. When you're ready, call the number on the back. We should talk about what you saw, before the last full moon. It's going to be in the sky at the carnival. Good day, Mr. Stephens."

She gracefully slid into the car then pulled across a small, purple, velvet curtain that was attached to the window as they drove off.

Daniel went home not paying any attention at first to the gobble-de-gook that his teacher had spun at him. He distracted himself by doing homework, reading, and playing **Monster Lair** on his computer. From time to time, his thoughts roamed back to the book, which he had thrown on his bed the minute he was in his bedroom. As he became bored of looking through his closet to put together the so-called costume that he technically lied about to Mrs. Vadoma to get her out of his way, the pressure, as well as the eager curiosity of his adolescent mind started to get to him. He decided to get it over with and look at the book.

This book couldn't be described in mere words. The cover was made of what may have been flesh, but the color of it was turquoise mixed with gold and black. The title on the book read: *THE MONTGOMERY SIDESHOW & CAGEHOUSE COMPANY RECORDS AND LAWS.*

Looking through it was like looking through a giant scrap book. Page one had been made up of tickets. They were the same three tickets the masters came across after they had first entered to the Dark Circus. The next numbers of pages were filled with pictures and the history of the freaks and animals that lived in the circus. Then there were three black and gold flyers stuck together. The first flyer depicted a picture of a man with turquoise skin, black hair, swords protruding from his arms, and fins protruding from his neck. This same man was hunched on his knees over the words: *The Dark Circus presents the Karloff Ray, Freak of Freaks* The second flyer was of a beautiful woman in a black corset, black net stockings, red, velvet tail coat, and spiked boots. She was holding a long whip while standing in front of a golden lion. Below her were the words: *The Dark Circus present Cassandra Castle, the Enchanting Tamer.* The third flyer was of the person Daniel had been hearing so much about in his dreams and from Mrs. Vadoma. It was a man dressed in a black and tuxedo a black top hat. He held open a black cape with one hand and a fanning out a deck of cards with the other hand. Below him, were the words: *The Dark Circus presents the Desmond Steinman, the Mystic Magician and Master of Mystery.*

The last sets of pages were very detailed, because they contained the history of the circus. The story read:

The boy known only as Desmond Steinman, who was estranged from everything and everyone in his small town, left his life behind to find another world where his unusual gifts would be seen as amazing and powerful. But, as he continued his quest for such a world, a dark one was watching. This stranger could see that Desmond was growing weary of demonstrating his magic solely to the humans close by and the gypsies that passed. At the moment when it could feel his power grow dormant, the dark one appeared to Desmond. It revealed itself as the Devil's Mistress, and it offered him a chance of a lifetime, the chance to create the world he so sought not just for him but many others that possessed the same gifts as he did. This mistress had also warned him that his world would open many doors between the realms of the living and dead; therefore, he would be encountered by creatures that breathed darkness. Their presence would not only increase his power, but would turn him into something dark as well. Desmond gladly accepted. Ever keeping the mistress's words in mind, Desmond had created such a place, and he named it the DARK CIRCUS... For many years, he kept the circus running. The ones who entered knew him as The Mystic Magician, while the ones who lived there: the freaks, the animals, and the gypsies who rejected him and whose queen was cursed and bound to the circus, called him the MASTER MAGICIAN. The more others who came to the circus, the stronger he became, which made the master decide that he had to share his power to relieve the burden and maintain balance. Only two of the six that attempted to prove themselves had succeeded. There was Cassandra, a woman with the skill to control all beasts with the command of her voice and the lash of her whip. She became the MASTER TAMER. There was Karloff, a man so unusual physically and mentally that the only word that could describe him would be freakish. Like a chameleon, he could take on the form of anyone or anything he wanted. When Desmond had given him the title of the MASTER FREAK, Karloff had sworn his loyalty, protection, and servitude to the Magician by embedding swords deep into his own flesh. It was the start of a wonderfully twisted friendship...

On the final page, which was the back cover of the book, were the laws of the circus written by the hand of Desmond himself.

- *The circus gates shall be open until the new day approaches.*
- *Tickets must be given to pass through the circus unharmed.*
- *No one may challenge the rule of the masters without just cause unless...* (the rest of this part was unfinished as if someone had taken a pencil and erased it)
- *All beasts must remain on the grounds and must agree to submit their will.*
- *They who sing and dance may wander the grounds and keep this written law; but they may not interfere with contrary magic.*
- *All performances or displays must be kept within the grounds.*
- *All performances from any creature of the circus must be guaranteed to entertain or risk the loss of their soul.*
- *Everyone shall attend the Harvest Festival.*

Daniel took one blow at a time. He told himself that he wasn't going to call Mrs. Vadoma, because he believed he deserved some answers that could only be given face-to-face. So, in the dead of night, he snuck out to return to that alley of insanity.

At first, he thought he would surprise his teacher for once and pop up when *she* didn't expect it or when she was caught off guard in her sleep. However, it wasn't too big of a surprise that when he arrived, she was there waiting for him on the bench across from the alley.

"You were supposed to call."

He shrugged his shoulders as a reply. Then she continued.

"Interesting book, wasn't it? It's been in my family for generations. And when I was a little girl, my mother told me that someday, I would give it back to the rightful owner."

"Why are you doing this? What does that book or anything have to do with me? And why did you call me Master Magician?"

"First thing's first. You tell me what you saw that night and I will tell you everything."

Chapter 10
Behind Closed Windows

DANIEL SAT NEXT TO Mrs. Vadoma on the bench. He took a deep breath and then described, in detail, everything he saw in her trailer about Madame Fate and her words that someone convinced the devil's mistress that he had been unworthy. Then he worked into the conversation, his feelings of late about the three new students, especially about Karl. He mentioned the dreams of Charlie. Normally, people who heard this type of conversation would probably direct Daniel to the nearest mental institution for intensive therapy sessions, but Mrs. Vadoma simply gave him a smile along with a pat on the back.

"I didn't realize exactly how fast things were being thrown out of whack, but our ancestors warned us that we should never underestimate the power of the darkness, especially when there are those so eager to have it."

"You know, you really should go in to theatre, because you're talking like someone out of a Shakespearian play."

"After my stomach-clenching experience of playing Juliet in the first grade, I haven't touched a Shakespearian play. But speaking of theatrical scenes, let me ask you something, Master Magician. Don't you think it was strange about the lighthouse falling? I'm sure you've heard by now that the police found balloons filled with explosives. I mean, don't get me wrong; we have crime like any other place in the world, but how many maniacs are running around with bombs in a small town like Spoonersville?"

"Well, I haven't had time to check out the local chat rooms on my computer." He jested.

"The point, Daniel, is that it's considered unusual even here. I think that someone was trying to get your's and the other masters' attention the same someone who was strong enough to send out magic that hasn't been used in a century to awaken my grandmother with visions of our ancestor. The school board, despite what has happened, has decided to let the Dean move the carnival across the way."

"To the empty lot?"

She responded with a nod and a pat on the back.

"Things are happening that can't be stopped. The only ones who can set them right are the descendants of Desmond, Cassandra, and Karloff. It's only because of them that the circus has been able to stay under control for as long as it has been. And it is because of their reputation that no one has dared to cross the line and make trouble for either side."

"So, what do you want me to do? I mean, I haven't even saved my notes for the geometry test next week; now you're telling me I have to save the world?"

"I want you to be yourself, the way you were before you became this person of denial. If the clown really has convinced the devil's mistress that you and your friends aren't fit to have the gifts you have, then it means big trouble for everyone..."

She reached for something inside of the tan bag next to her feet, "...here... you forgot these the other night. See you tomorrow night."

Mrs. Vadoma went back to that alley meeting up with the little girl Daniel had seen many times. What she gave to him was the deck of cards he originally owned before he sold them to Joey at the joke shop, who in turn had sold it to an old lady.

October 31st...The day of the carnival finally came, and all the students were in a buzz, except for our three friends. Daniel showed that he was focused with other thoughts from the way he shuffled the cards of his old deck. Kyle and C.A. were moping around, remembering their little spat from the day before. Although they may have felt a little awkward about it, the three of them rendezvoused at the lion statue. C.A. was the first to break the ice.

"Hey."

"Hey..." followed Daniel.

"Yeah, hey." entered Kyle.

"What time were you guys gonna go tonight? Or were you guys gonna go tonight?" C.A. asked.

"Are you kidding, this is the biggest thing to hit town since the invention of dog food," Kyle replied.

"Hahahaha." She laughed sarcastically.

"Andrew said he might go. I haven't seen him all day; I'm gonna go by his house later."

"Well, if he is definitely going, then you know Karl and Diana will probably be there, too." Daniel spoke with a distrustful tone in his voice.

"You make it sound like a bad thing."

"Maybe it is. Look, I have something to tell you guys. A lot of strange things have been going on. I mean, like my dreams, Mrs. Vadoma, Mr. Up-Chuck, and now Karl and his friends. Did you know that Mrs. Vadoma is an honest to heck gypsy...?"

"A gypsy? I heard she was an alcoholic." Kyle said.

"I heard she was one of those exotic belly dancers from Vegas." C.A. agreed in her own way.

Then, Daniel re-entered the conversation, "...I got a feeling something big is going to happen tonight. And that it might involve... *Charlie.*"

C.A. and Kyle faced one another, almost uninterested in anything that Daniel may have had to say.

"Houdini, the clown is dead. We saw it ourselves." Kyle explained in a low tone.

"Then why do I have these dreams? I think they're a warning of some kind, and it has something to do with Mr. Up-Chuck. The other day I found this napkin or handkerchief, and it reminded me of the clown."

"Well, unless you know a way to recover from a giant lion eating you in one gulp, I'm going to have to agree with Freak here. What's really going on, Daniel? Is it just that you don't want to hang out with Karl and his friends?"

"Well, I'm sorry if it makes me look like some sort of odd ball because I don't want to be around your new friends. And why do you guys want to spend all day and night with them anyway? You've only known them for a few days."

"Oh, don't act so innocent, Daniel. We've seen the way you've been getting all cozy with Diana..." forcibly spoke the green monster, showing its way on Christy-Anne's face, "...the way you act when she puts her hand on your shoulder or when she smiles at you. You look like an idiot."

"What!" Daniel responded in full shock, "... What are you talking about? I haven't done anything."

"Oh, please that's what all you men say."

"*You men?* What other men have you been see?"

"And so, we conclude another Spanish soap opera," Kyle announced in a deep romantic Hispanic voice.

"Oh, shut up Freak!" snapped C.A.

"Hey, don't yell at me, miss zookeeper. You know, I'm surprised they would be interested in you at all since the only friends you've ever made can only say chirp-chirp and squeak-squeak."

"Oh yeah, well the only friends you'll ever make..."

"Guys, enough!" intruded Daniel. Words were flying faster than a race car on the tracks. While the young masters argued amongst themselves, Mr. Up-Chuck was watching a few feet away from the right side of the janitor shed. It was a wonder if he could even hear what they were saying at all over his own heavy breathing that he was doing through his nostrils.

"Come on now. We're all friends, here, and we have been ever since we could crawl. Of course, in your case, Kyle, you have a tendency to jump everywhere like a frog."

The three of them laughed. They couldn't explain what brought out the things they said to each other, so they collected themselves before saying another word.

"Sorry you guys." Christy- Anne apologized first.

"Yeah, me, too." said Daniel.

"What he said and then some." said Kyle.

The three laughed one more time to make sure that the tension was cleared between them.

"So, I guess we'll just see each other when we see each other."

"Great." Kyle gestured with a salute before rushing off with his skateboard.

As they went their separate ways, Daniel felt once again, the sharp, painful flashes crawling up the back of his neck to the middle of his brain. He could sense two things: For one there was the nightmares he had been having for many nights about his friends in the Dark Circus forms practically dead on the floor of the arena. For another there was the phrase that continuously repeated itself over and over by the female voice he was now certain belonged to Madame Fate.

"*You were right not to trust me.*"

He snapped back to reality at the sound of the horn of a random car passing by over a bump. Daniel wanted to further warn his friends about what was coming, but he decided that he should go home not only to get ready for the carnival, but to prepare for a fight like his teacher had warned him. Whatever was going to happen, he could feel that tonight's excitement would only trigger it. After all, the plans changed from the carnival to taking place near the recently ruined lighthouse to the carnival taking place in the empty lot across from the lighthouse, that same empty lot with the black gate.

Kyle decided to go to 1717 Big Top Drive to visit with his friend, Andrew. Of course, he wasn't aware that he wouldn't be going alone. In the brief time that he had known Andrew, and in their so-called friendship or shaky bond that they had recently formed, Kyle would just go over to his house, knock on the door, and they would already be playing on the various game systems. However, the moment that he jumped off his skateboard, he could see and hear shadows. Coming up the steps of the patio of Andrew's house, reaching for the knob of the front door, Kyle saw, once again, the shadows of Henry and Clowey. They looked at him with disappointment.

He wanted to speak to them, until the door opened suddenly. Andrew, looked as if he hadn't slept for a millennium, with his long hair muffled and his eyes appearing only slightly gold instead of all gold like they were when he first jumped on Kyle. The intensity of the moment made Kyle's nails grow a little longer although he couldn't tell that it was happening.

"Well, if it isn't the freak boy." said Andrew.

"So, what's the deal? You feeling sick or something?"

"No." he answered as if the questions Kyle asked were nothing or as if he simply didn't care.

"Then why'd you miss school? And for that matter why do you look like the after shot of a bad commercial?"

"Wow, that was clever. Look, buddy boy, we're not married, so I don't have to tell you everything that goes on in my life."

"Whatever, I was just asking"

"Don't you have to go back to your punk master?"

"What does that mean?"

"Oh, come on. Your friends call you a freak, but all you are is some lackey who likes to pretend that he's hardcore. Honestly, I don't know what that wash upped magician, Desmond, saw in your ancestor, Karloff. You don't have what it takes to be a freak not if you keep obeying and tagging along with the two of them like some dog."

"Watch your mouth,"

"Oh yeah?"

"Yeah, before I rip it off and feed it to the sharks. And I don't know who you think Karloff is to me, but I'll personally send you into the white light to meet him face to face."

"Oh, I'm real scared of you. By the way, you can't dance Cotton Eye Joe to save your life."

Andrew slammed the door hard into Kyle's face. As he angrily stomped his way down the steps of the patio ready to turn the corner on his skate-board, Kyle was stopped in his tracks by Henry, whose expression changed from looking at him in a wrongful way to pointing out a spot around the side of Andrew's house.

Since there was nothing better to do (thanks to his maybe soon former friend, Andrew's, attitude problem), he followed his instincts, as well as the shadows to the other side. Coming around, he could hear the house phone ringing and Andrew yelling to his parents to let them know that he would take it. The room where he was had the window closed, but even closed windows couldn't stop Kyle from listening in on the conversation. He had bent on his knees low enough to not be seen. For some reason, being that close to the floor suddenly triggered the Master Freak's skin to stretch out from his cheekbones up to the top of his head. It was only slightly painful, but it was strong enough to make him touch where the pain was moving towards, which was the back of his ears. He moved his fingers across them he soon realized that his ears morphed into pointed tips. Their size and shape created a strong sound that echoed better than the sonar of a submarine. He could hear everything that Andrew was saying.

"Diana? What do you want...? Yeah, the freak just left. He'll show up like the trained sidekick he is. What about the tamer... Good... Karl said we'll catch up with you at the carnival tonight. He's on his way over here, right now."

Kyle made a slight jester to reposition himself against the wall, but all his moving caused him to bump into a planter next to his feet, and the rattling did not go unnoticed to Andrew. He turned his head towards the window, not getting any whiplash. He knew he wasn't alone. He told Diana, "... I got to go. See you tonight, Serpent Girl."

Andrew gently put down the phone. He made it seem as if he exited out into the other rooms of the house, but unknown to our long haired, flee-infested, big-man of the world friend, Kyle wasn't fooled. His ears were too good a warning. He knew that Andrew was softly treading on the floor, getting ready to come up to the window for a surprise attack.

Andrew unlocked the top hinges. He slowly raised the bottom of the window, hardly causing any squeaks. Kyle started to breathe in and out of his nose. He thought of what to do or say the second Andrew would see him, but he didn't have to think much longer. The second that the window went up Kyle stood up, but he didn't look like himself. His Master Freak impulse helped him transform in the shape of...

"Damn, Karl! I thought you were a Russian spy or something."

That's right... Kyle changed his appearance to Karl, and he went along with the charade that he was Andrews another friend.

"What took you so long?" Andrew asked.

Dark Circus: The Astonishing Return

"I had to wait for the freak to leave." Kyle replied, attempting to play it cool.

"Don't worry; he won't be back anytime soon. I don't see why we just don't get rid of the player haters. I mean, they're weak right now."

Kyle wasn't sure what to say. For the most part, he responded to Andrew's questions with a nod or a shrugged shoulder. They prattle about, talking for fifteen minutes. Even though Kyle was in Karl's form, Andrew didn't seem to give up as much information as most people would when they're around familiar faces.

"So, what did Diana want?"

"She just wanted to let us know she's on her way over to the carnival grounds. She's gonna hitch a ride with the tamer. I don't know about the Magician. He's been talking to that teacher, too much. I saw them in the alley a little while ago. You think he'll show up?"

"Oh, I'm sure he'll pop up eventually, like a rabbit from a hat. Isn't that what magicians do for their opening bid?"

Andrew laughed. "That's a good one. I don't remember you being this funny."

"I got to go."

"What do you mean? It's almost time for the party. You're my ride."

"It'll just take a couple of minutes. I'll be back. Don't be such a girl."

Instead of exiting out the front door, Kyle chose to leave the way he originally entered. Andrew never removed his gaze from him. After Kyle left Andrew immediately grabbed the phone to dial the real Karl according to the name that appeared on the caller id. It almost seemed as though he immediately knew that it wasn't really Karl with whom he was talking.

Chapter 11
Rise of the Black Gate

MEANWHILE, TIME WAS moving on, as well as the whole town up to the lighthouse grounds. Before he decided to leave, Daniel was in his room. He didn't have much of a costume planned. He was going to call Kyle to borrow some sort of attire that could make a statement; but again, he hadn't seen or heard from Kyle in a while since in front of the school. He called C.A. as well to see if she was alright, but according to her father, she already left with Diana. Things were getting worse by the second.

Daniel wore a black t-shirt, black pants, and a red, puff-up snow jacket that a person would see in a sports store. More words and flashes from the past appeared before his eyes; although the pain wasn't as severe as before. He could hear Madame Fate's voice, but he saw that it was Mrs. Vadoma that spoke to him.

"I *shall be with you young master...*"

He walked to the door shoving his hands into his jacket pockets. As his hands moved around the interior, Daniel could see that he forgotten something... his cards. Although he couldn't remember where he had placed them while he was getting ready, Daniel didn't panic like most people do who lose valuable things. He didn't have to tear up the room. He just observed it left to right with a normal glance. Then when he glanced back right to leave, his eyes were focusing everything in slow motion. He extended his right arm with his palm of his hand facing up. Then he said,

"Abra Kadabra..."

just to get a kick. Of course, these words didn't work, and nothing was happening. He moved a little further outside his bedroom door then made another attempt to mystically retrieve his cards. The term, BEWARE, entered his mind and he recalled what could happen if the word was said backwards.

"ERAWEB."

The cards came to him as if they were attached to a thin, retractable wire attached to Daniel's arms. He gripped the cards, giving them a hard glance. Then he told himself,

"It's official. I've lost my mind."

As he left, not everything remained still in his room. By the window was the famous book that Mrs. Vadoma had gifted to Daniel. The breeze that pressed against its glass resurfaced. Like a great hand, it tugged the spine of book inch by inch, until it finally fallen to the ground. Maybe it was going to follow Daniel to the carnival.

It was such a festive affair that night. Cars were so jammed together that many people parked on the sidewalks. The citizens of Spoonersville were having the time of their lives. Small children practically ripped their parents' hands or legs off trying to get them to spend their money on the cotton candy, popcorn, balloons, and other décor that was designed based on the Morgan Hill High School logo and colors of burgundy and gold.

Haunting lamps flowed gracefully against the poles from which they were hung as they lead up the spiral road of the average sized hill, where the Old Bailey Lighthouse stood. Police were stationed in front of the lighthouse, blocking it off as best they could with the yards of yellow tape.

Daniel thought, as he came closer to the entrance of that lot, that the gates would be just as black as before. But it turned out to be just another rusty, old gate. The memories kept appearing to Daniel since the second he entered the carnival. He could hear something spread at the bottom of his shoes. Before going any further, he put his hand on the nearest stone wall and noticed the dust attached to it. It was colored black and gold.

The moment that he looked up, Daniel could see the little gypsy girl. She was doing a cute job at the carnival by passing out tickets to people. When she saw Daniel, she ran by his side to give him one of the tickets, and then she quickly ran back. He flipped it, thinking he would see the initials *DIS* as he had seen them once on the tickets that were left for the three on the wooden stand in front of the entrance to the circus. Then it occurred to him that one of the laws inside of the book mentioned that tickets must be given to assure a person's safety through the dark circus.

The atmosphere of that night couldn't have been measured. While Daniel did indeed move about the scene, C.A. attempted to play the efficient role by checking off the list of everything she and Diana bought. The girls passed one another items from several boxes as they were sporting the Morgan Hill T-shirts. Kyle was there, but he tried to not be noticed, at least in the sense for someone like Kyle. He searched over heads and underneath and between legs to find Daniel and C.A.

Even Frederick, who disappeared for a while, tried to find CA. He was in such a hurry that he didn't even make a grab for the dozens of peanut shells as he zigzagged by people's feet. He eventually found his way to her by hiding in a small crack inside of the drink stand, which was stationed before a dirt-smudged poster of a Ferris Wheel.

"Everything seems to be going great." said Diana.

"Yeah. I didn't think I would like being up here again after what happened last time." C.A. explained.

"What happened last time?"

Frederick started to squeak. C.A. hesitated to respond to Diana's question, because she knew that even if she did tell someone the truth about what happened three years ago... well... you get the idea. She could also feel that something whispered harshly to her mind making her stop from bringing out the words. Frederick continued to squeak, but he was not getting any reaction from C.A.

Although Mrs. Vadoma stayed with her musician friends, who played a few nights before, her eyes seemed to be wandering with the same seriousness her students had seen from her in class. She was observing every inch of the carnival with her hands held behind her back. She may have been acting as the parental chaperon by occasionally noting the kids; however, it appeared that her attention was set on finding someone. It wasn't Daniel. She knew that he was there since the little gypsy girl had returned to tell her, so no, it couldn't have been Daniel.

Having no luck, her expression turned from serious to minor fear.

Looking down from the large hill beside the lot, where the waters of a gray sea had beaten against the rocks below it, was Mr. Up-Chuck wearing his magician's cape and carrying three other items. The first was the seal horn he purchased from Joey. It was gripped tightly by Up-Chuck's tartar- stained teeth. The second item was the long, oval mirror he had dragged out from his shrine in the janitor's shed all the way to the top of that hill. The third item was the gramophone also from the shed. He waited until the clouds completely repelled the light of the constant full moon, the moment when everyone could feel a chill spread through their veins. Charlie appeared in the mirror as vapor, ready to command his loyal servant to do his bidding.

"IT'S TIME! IT'S TIME! HAHAHAHAHAHAHAHAHAHAHAHAH AHA!"

The clown's laugh echoed across the land. People searched all about them to see from where it was coming. Timothy Porter cried,

"Mommy, what's that?"

"*HAHAHAHAHAHAHAHAHAHAHAH AHAHAHAHAHAHA!*"

The sound continued to rave. Then someone else shouted.

"Hey look up there!"

Heads had quickly shifted to the hill.

"Up-Chuck?" Kyle expressed with surprise.

Mr. Up-Chuck activated the gramophone and its twisted music. Like one of Kyle's mangled marionette puppets he started to dance to the sour notes as if he had no control over his own pudgy body. He was imitating the way that Charlie was moving in the mirror. Every step repeated: shoulders up, elbows out, knees bent, slap the face... 1, 2, 3... shoulders up, elbows out, knees bent, slap the face... 1, 2, 3. On the last go around of this insane routine, Mr. Up-Chuck froze entirely, except for his right arm. It moved like a clock hand grabbing the seal horn.

Miss Sophia Carter softly jabbered from the side of her mouth to Miss Melanie James.

"What the heck is he doing? The Macarena?"

"I don't know, but for eight bucks a ticket the choreography doesn't seem well planned out."

Mr. Up-Chuck took the horn lifting it straight in the air. He squeezed it three times as if he was sounding an alarm. The air shifted bringing rough winds that were strong enough to make bodies wobble. He squeezed the horn again, now sucking force into the bottom causing it to expand. People were trying to hold on to whatever was secured to the ground.

Kyle curled himself up into a ball. Then he tried to crawl against the wind on all fours so that his body wouldn't take off. But when it seemed like his two legs wouldn't be enough to sustain him Kyle could feel something trying to burst out the bottom sides of his hips. The further he went the more aggressive it felt. Finally peering down, he could see that what popped out of his sides were two legs, covered in striped stockings and girl shoes. Even though he couldn't help widening his eyes in shock, Kyle took his nerves by the neck and continued to crawl. Christy-Anne and Diana hid under the stand. They were fighting the boxes that bum rushed them to the face. C.A could hear panicked squeaking and saw that Frederick was holding on from her shoe lace like a flying flag. She grabbed and stuffed him in her pants pocket faster than firemen put out a fire. Daniel was the only one of the three who did not stay to the ground. As he gazed up at Mr. Up-Chuck in a meditative state, he started to hover above the ground but only by a foot. It was as if he had let the wind pick him up.

Mr. Up-Chuck squeezed the horn again. Instead of keeping it up in the air as he done, he pointed it to the mirror. The vapor image of Charlie was pulled out of the reflection into the horn, and the mirror shattered into dozens of fragments that barely missed the people below. When it was completely full, Mr. Up-Chuck turned the instrument on himself. He squeezed it for a final time, receiving a harsh gust that nearly tore him apart. His body was shaking like a rattle even when he dropped the horn. The color of his face become powder white; his eyes had been painted over with black eye shadow as well as his lips, which were covered in black lipstick.

He went from being a bald man to being an even fatter man with crazy red hair. His clothes had blended with his yellow and black spotted socks. His teeth were sharp and jagged. And then... And then...

"*SURPRISE! HELLO KIDDIES! WELCOME TO THE MAIN EVENT. HAHAHAHAHAHA!*" entered the voice of you know who

Mr. Up-Chuck horribly transformed into Charlie.

"*GOOD DAY MY SPOONTONIANS, ARE YOU READY FOR A FRIGHT?! FOR CHARLIE HAS GREAT PLANS FOR ALL YOU TONIGHT. A TRIO AMONGST YOU BELIEVED THEY HAD STOPPED ME, BUT SUCH FOOLISHNESS WILL NOW PROVE EVER SO COSTLY. I WILL HAVE JUSTICE FOR THEIR TREACHEROUS CRIME AND REGAIN THAT WHICH WAS RIGHTFULLY MINE...*"

Daniel came to his feet, but still maintained a focused stare with the clown. Christy-Anne, with the help of the edge of the stand, slowly rose to her feet to also meet

Charlie's eyes. Kyle like, a grasshopper, flipped over on his legs, which had returned to just being two legs instead of four, and bounced up like a stiff board also looking Charlie dead in the face.

"... *SO, WELCOME, AGAIN, YOUNG MASTERS. BE PREPARED TO FEAST YOUR EYES. DARK CIRCUS, LIVE AGAIN, AND BLACK GATES... ARISE!*"

The ground reacted by cracking and quaking. One group of people was on their feet, running towards the only exit as best as they could while the other group tried climbing on chairs or trees to avoid being dropped into a possible, large hole. But the cracks didn't open. They traveled in the direction everyone else had been running. No one stood a chance of leaving, because the once rusty, old gate had been knocked away by a large, black hand that sprung from the ground and morphed itself into a new gate. Soon the setting became all too familiar for Daniel and his friends.

Chapter 12
Showing off Talent

THE MASSES HUDDLED tightly together in fear. No one knew what to do. Mrs. Vadoma tried to take direction by standing on top of a box to get a better view of everyone. Then she yelled and waved her hands about to gain their attention,

"Everyone! Everyone, please be calm! You're only giving the clown what he wants. Your fear is fueling his power."

Soon, the sound of wild animals echoed. Some believed they were surrounded by baboons, they were being chased by elephants, or that they were next to a vicious tiger or a wolf. The concession stands and games had been transformed into topsy-turvy tents, colored with orange and black stripes. The poster that was behind Christy-Anne, the one of the Ferris Wheel, peeled its way off the wall. Once it hit the ground, the cracks that had come from the direction of the gate zipped to the poster creating an opening wide enough for the image of the Ferris Wheel to rise up and become a reality. There were also the enormous rollercoaster and other rides that sprung up like bed springs. Just as Charlie had commanded... the Dark Circus was alive, once more. This time, everyone was trapped within its gothic wonder.

Eventually, Daniel spotted Kyle. They screamed to hear each other over the squeals of everyone else.

"Dude, you came!"

"What can I say? I have no life!"

"Where's C.A.?"

"I don't know; I can't find her anywhere! What do we do?"

"We need to find her and get everyone out of here."

"I'm open to suggestions."

Just then, Charlie swooped down from the hill towards the boys at an incredible speed, his diabolic grin spewing green venom the faster he went. Feeling the clown's attack, a card falls from the inside of Daniel's jacket sleeve into his hand. Its edges were sharp and jagged. He was about to throw it at Charlie when suddenly, the clown was knocked out of the way by a ball of fire as big as a fist. Sadly, the clown blocked it with the use of his magic cape. The boys looked in the direction they believed the attack came from. Through the rushing citizens, they could see that positioned in a surfer type way was Karl, who soon pulled out his black and orange ping pong balls, juggled them in a crisscross pattern, then threw them at Charlie, again. As these balls were being thrown, they had grown and been set on fire.

"*SO, THE JUGGLER WANTS TO PLAY? OH, WHAT AN EXCITING DAY!*" Charlie responded, recovering from Karl's bombardment. He took another dive only this time it was towards Karl. But Daniel had stepped in to repay the favor by using his cards to topple Charlie over.

The boys ran to Karl.

"Thanks," Karl said.

"Don't mention it," Daniel said.

"How do you do that?" Kyle inquired.

"Come on, the girls are this way." Karl led the way. The boys quickly followed.

After seeing the Ferris Wheel come to life, Diana and Christy-Anne jumped out of their little zone. Diana performed an impressive dive into round off jump as C.A. did an equally impressive cartwheel out while keeping Frederick in her pocket. As soon as Charlie caught sight of them, he pulled the inside of his cape to his chest then back out to magically send out these moldy greenish-gray pies, topped with whipped cream and a cherry on its curl. Diana rose from the ground completely unafraid of the deadly pies. In fact, her eyes seem to momentarily glow the same blue that was in her hair. She put her teeth together and started to hiss through them like a serpent. As the pies were coming closer to hitting her face, C.A. saw that Diana's left leg stretched out very thinly and wobbly. She struck the pies away with a kick like a flyswatter.

"What!" C.A. exclaimed.

Frederick made his way out of the pocket. As he made his escape, C.A. fell to the dirt. Before pushing herself completely up with her elbows, she could see to her right one of the shattered fragments of glass from the mirror Mr. Up-Chuck used. However, within her own reflection, she could see a familiar face. It was a beautiful golden, fur-covered face. It was the lion (the same lion who helped C.A. realize her power as the Master Tamer and had swallowed Charlie on the other side of the ring of fire). He was lying on his side the same way that she was on the ground with his stomach practically gone and his tale barely moving to reach out to his master.

"Oh my..." Christy-Anne gasped under her breath.

Then over both the girls' heads, descending from incredible heights, was Andrew, his yellow eyes set and his hair sprawled wildly out was ready to come at Charlie just as he had come at Kyle that day by the river.

"Took you long enough." hissed Diana.

"Don't tell me you're done showing off all your talents, serpent girl. I was expecting a lot more." Andrew snobbishly replied.

"Remind me to insult your mother later."

"*SO NOW THE DOGGY WANTS TO PLAY? THIS TRULY IS A SPECIAL DAY, AND MY SIX TROUBLES WILL SOON BE SENT AWAY!*"

"Shut up and scream, clown!" Andrew's voice almost had a growl to it.

He charged, like a predator, at full speed towards Charlie. His heart was beating fast as he went down to slide on his knees. He moved his hands back to give himself enough force to slash Charlie's legs. Fortunately for all of them the slash hurts the clown, but it didn't destroy him. Charlie returned to the air to heal himself as Daniel, Kyle, Karl, Diana, and C.A. all gather.

"Come on we got to move now!" Daniel yelled.

The kids were now running with the crowd being knocked about. People were still at the gate, trying to pry it open. Even the police on the other side couldn't open it with the Jaws of Life from the fire truck. The officers that weren't helping with the gate aimed their firearms at Charlie. But all their shots did, was make a lot of noise. None of them had even grazed the clown's skin. When Charlie's wounds recovered, he turned his attention on Spoonersville's finest. He gave them his evil smile and attacked them with the ongoing, twisted magic he was dishing out before. It was pie frenzy. Deadly whipped cream covered the cars and signs along the streets. They were hitting the officer's directly in the face as well as the back of their heads, their stomach, and their sides. In fact, the impact was so effective that when the pies had tipped to the side of their heads, the expressions on the officers were like Charlie's own grin. Their bodies also seemed to stop moving. The legendary Bozo would have been so proud at the sight of this.

Chapter 13
Return to the Big Top

THE KIDS REMAINED a short distance behind everyone else at the gate.

"It's like the end of the world," Karl said.

"We'll never get out that way." Diana then spoke.

"Why does that sound all too familiar to me?" entered Kyle.

"We have to do something to get these people out of here." Christy-Anne pointed out the obvious

"Not to mention ourselves." Andrew ended the conversation.

Daniel looked around to find a solution. Thankfully, he remembered the hill above them. Right in front of the hill was an old, stone wall that could easily be brought down with the right force.

"Karl..." he says, "...throw a fireball at that wall."

Then all of them had understood the idea that Daniel had.

"You got it."

Karl went before the structure and threw one of his ping pong balls. It made a ball of fire on impact with the wall, forcing it to crumble. Then Daniel did his part by sliding off his jacket and taking the card deck in his hand to the opening. First, he looked at the crowds of people at the gate, who were obviously panicked and oblivious about what was going all around them, to observe their frightened expressions. Then he refocused his attention on the hole, flung his arms out, and said,

"ERAWEB!"

The winds came to help him by making the cards fly into formation. Everyone could see that these cards were becoming one and had started to form a ladder.

"Everyone! This way!" Daniel screamed.

The rush to the hole was the size of a tidal wave. Daniel, Karl, and the rest waited for the chance to climb over. When the chance had occurred to them Daniel had heard a different screaming from one of the tents. He turned his eyes to see that Mrs. Vadoma was tugging and pulling herself from the grip of Charlie, who had Mrs. Vadoma hovering a foot above the ground.

"Let go of me! Let go of me, you psycho!" she ranted repeatedly.

The little gypsy girl had tried to help her by grabbing Mrs. Vadoma's feet, but her little body wasn't strong enough to manipulate gravity to her advantage. Daniel's friends were trying to get him to move along with them.

"Houdini, let's go!" Kyle called.

"You guys go ahead; I'll catch up." he responded calmly.

"We're not leaving you!" C.A. said.

"Just go; I'll be right behind you." he instructed while running in a heroic fashion.

C.A. and Kyle looked at each other thinking to themselves, **why us**? They took the hint from their friend by who was trying to play the hero. The other three reached out to them with a similar plea for getting out of there.

"What are you guys doing?!" Diana screamed, really pretending to be concerned about the young masters.

"What did I tell you, Andrew? People who can't mind their own business, that's who I hang out with." Kyle explained.

"Be sure not to get yourself killed. I'm not done with you, yet" Andrew replied.

C.A. and Kyle followed Daniel towards certain death, or at least it appeared to be certain death. The other three immediately glanced at each other as if they had expected all of this to happen.

Galloping faster than Paul Revere, Daniel was out in front. He came around the corner of the tent, glad to see that the little girl had remained on the ground, hanging on to Mrs. Vadoma's foot with her small elbows. He used his weight to make a jump for Mrs. Vadoma's legs to try to get her down.

As Kyle ran, he could feel a tingle the same pain he felt earlier during the harsh wind, when the four extra components burst from the side of his hips. The pain was now moving along his arms. It given him the urge to stretch them out, and soon, black feathers had sprung from his skin. He used them to take flight, leaving behind C.A. even more confused. However, returning to her side was Frederick, pumping his body back and forth at full speed with her. He wanted to join them, but she commanded him to stay back to make sure the opening at the wall was still there for them to escape. He did as she telepathically commanded him to do.

Daniel knelt the left side of his body to secure the little girl back on her feet. After he was sure that she was alright, he put his attention towards the direction where Charlie hovered Mrs. Vadoma. Luckily wherever he was going, Kyle made it to the clown before he could float another inch. And when it seemed that they were both about to make contact something occurred to make them both fall straight down. It was almost like they had lost power.

"*AH PHEWY!*" Charlie exclaimed.

"Great." Kyle moaned.

Falling back down loosened Charlie's grip on Mrs. Vadoma. C.A. and Daniel caught up to them. They could see that Charlie was breathing a little heavier and that Kyle kept touching his head. In fact, the more times he patted it, the colors of Kyle's eyes turned black and then returned to normal. Daniel had got up and marched towards the Charlie, pulling out the only card that wasn't being used for the ladder at the hole in the wall. The card with the red "X".

"NOT SO FAST, MY MAGIAN FRIEND. THIS IS HARDLY THE END."

"Oh yeah? Well, I got something here that says differently." Daniel raised the card above himself, and as an instinctive reaction, it morphed into the vicious red blade sword with the black handle. Another thing about the blade was that it appeared to be burnt. It was almost as if it had been through a hundred battles.

Suddenly, the ground started to quake, again, creating an opening practically a few inches away from them. Rising from its crumbling entrance was an object too familiar to Daniel. It was a large, rusty machine, shaded the color of green with purple chariot wheels; the word **BEWARE** was displayed clearly on the front, and there were three windows (covered by curtains) that made up its side. It was the Fortune Telling Machine of Madame Fate. The curtains inside of the machine parted, revealing that mechanical gypsy made of wood with her purple, glittered clothes, her magnificent scarf above her head, and the forest green paint over her eyes.

Mrs. Vadoma was in complete shock as she looked upon this thing. Then she quickly recognized that it was her great ancestor., the ancestor of her mother's ancestor. She was terrified because Mrs. Vadoma had noticed that Madame Fate was softly speaking in their native Russian tongue, and because of the way she kept putting her hands together in prayer then touching the top of her head with the tips of her fingers, Mrs. Vadoma knew what spell was being cast all around them.

The machine began to wobble off its hinges as light built from the center of Madame Fate's crystal ball. Then... she spokes.

"Enough!" she said, "... the mistress, she comes."

"What mistress?" C.A. asked, staying close by Mrs. Vadoma like an infant to calm herself down.

"The Devil's Mistress," Daniel whispered under his breath while taking a step forward.

From behind Madame Fate's machine emerged a dark-robed, female-shaped figure. The bottom of her face was the only thing that was revealed to them. Her nails scratched the surface of the green paint of the fortunetelling machine. This person radiated nothing but pure evil. The negative forces were so strong that Kyle, C.A., the little girl, and Mrs. Vadoma moved back the more this woman came towards them. Daniel was the only one who hadn't a clue as to why he wasn't moving along with them. Even Charlie wanted to move, but observing the others' reaction to whoever this creature was too good to miss.

Within inches of Daniel's face, the robed stranger revealed her full face. Indeed, the stranger was a woman and a most enticing woman to look at. Her brown eyes were hypnotizing. Her lips were fire red. Her hair was long, smooth, and shiny as black pearls from a rare oyster. She circled Daniel, trying to enchant him with her charms. Of course, Christy-Anne, ever being the non-jealous type, flung herself over by Daniels side to interrupt the mysterious woman's gaze.

Mrs. Vadoma rushed over to the kids. She knew who this person was as well. She even spoke her name with frustration and anger.

"Galena!" she shouted.

The woman smiled.

"Who's Galena?" Kyle now inquired.

"She is the Devil's Mistress, a witch who was once the sister of our ancestor until it was discovered that she was dealing with black magic. So, she convinced Desmond, the Mystic Magician, to help her curse my ancestor to live within that mechanical contraption for eternity."

"Are you kidding me?" CA asked in a high pitch tone.

"I assure you Master Tamer. This is no joke." spoke Galena, "These are very serious matters. And for the record, little Trisha, it is nice to see you, as well. Maybe your _fate_ will not be so bonding as my dear sister's," She bowed her head to be comforting.

"Oh great, so you and Madame Fate are sisters, now?" Daniel shrugged.

"Well, I can relate to being annoyed with your sister. I got double the trouble at home, myself." Kyle commented slightly sarcastic.

"Not now Freak!" CA commanded.

"You've been using Madame Fate to send me all those nightmares, haven't you? And you're the one who brought him back, aren't you?"

Charlie rolled over to answer Daniel's questions in his annoying fashion

"*THIS IS TRUE; I CAN-NOT LIE. THE MISTRESS WAS WILLING TO HERE MY CRY. THAT OVERGROWN CAT HAD TROUBLE DIGESTING. SHE LENDED HER HANDS TO PULL OUT THE NEXT BEST THING.*"

The mistress waltzed over to Charlie's side, towering over him almost as if she was hinting that he was not entirely off the hook. He responded by shaking on the inside. She bent down to touch the cape that Charlie was wearing. She rubbed the material through the tips of her fingers as if she was curious. She didn't say anything. All she did was smile back, but even that proved more frightening to the clown than his own smile.

She walked, with everyone's eyes focused on her, towards the machine. Gently, she brushed her hair back to pull on a black string around her neck. She lifted from the inside of her robe, a large, golden ticket that was attached to the string. She placed the object inside of the slot on the machine, which said: Insert Tickets. The machine rattled and spat out of control, making echoes that banged and clashed. The mistress stepped back only three steps and lifted her arms with the sleeves of her robes hanging and flowing with the wind that has followed Daniel nonstop on this adventure. Her eyes, which were once so beautifully brown, glowed red. She spoke the word,

"ERA WEB!!"

Once again, the ground opened from the cracks of the endless shaking. The light of Madame Fate's crystal ball got brighter and hotter just from the sight of its power. They all shielded their eyes. Her wooden mouth opened widely. Instead of words, there came the sound of more broken music. It was going *dah dah dadadadah dah dah dah dah dah dah dadadadah dah dah dah dah da dededy dah dededy.*

At the end of the song, long sheets of black and orange rose from the cracks, swirling together to form the same circus tent the young masters were in when they had confronted Charlie three years ago, Everyone, except for Galena, was flabbergasted at the sight; even Kyle, who always played the façade of a tough guy, felt fear in his legs.

"Come now, young masters. As the clown mentioned... this is far from over."

Chapter 14
The Trial

CHARLIE WAS THE FIRST to follow Galena inside. His mouth was still dripping a happy, green slime. Daniel looked to his friends, and even the little gypsy girl who was clutching tightly onto his right hand, for the okay to proceed. In fact, they all stayed close together, with Daniel leading in front, Kyle and CA watching the back, and Mrs. Vadoma in the middle. There were large, burgundy-red, velvet curtains at the tent's entrance that had closed abruptly behind them. The sound of the closing made an echo like a cell door being slammed shut.

Coming closer to the inside, they couldn't see anything because there was no light. In fact, it was harder to see if the Devil's Mistress and Charlie were still ahead of them. Soon, Daniel could feel the rustle of dirt underneath his shoes, like the gold and black dust he felt coming into the lot. One more step from the gang instantly sparked fire into these tilted, silver torches hovering above them without a wall. They could all see that they were standing in the dirt arena of the tent.

The audience bleachers surrounded the arena, with a silent and abnormal crowd of creatures to occupy them. Suddenly, C.A. stopped breathing as she looked a little further to her left. She could see that her old friend (the magnificent, golden lion) lay on the side of the arena as he had been in the reflection of the mirror she seen on the ground when Charlie attacked with his insides spewing out and his body split in half. Tears rolled down her cheeks as she ran to him. His eyes were barely open.

"Well look whose back." He struggled to telepathically say to her mind.

"What have you gotten yourself into now, you stupid cat?" she asked tearing up even more with every word.

Also, to the left of them were many familiar faces to Kyle. He had either seen shadows of or had morphed himself into most of them. These were the famous freaks. They looked to their Master Freak in admiration and praise although they were not allowed to make any jester to support him while in the presence of the mistress.

At the center of the arena, was a throne that would have fit in any renaissance fair. It was made of black, marble stone. The cushions of its seat and its back were covered in midnight blue. The top edges of the chair curved upward like the branches of a tree, and brightly colored streamers of dark purple and orange hung along the sides.

The mistress took her rightful place at the throne. She gestured Daniel and his friends with a wave of her hand.

"Shall the Heirs of Karloff Ray, Cassandra Castle, and Desmond Steinman step before me to claim their innocence?"

Patiently, after she asked the question the boys went to CA who was still at the lion's side trying to wipe away her tears. They comforted her with a hand on her back and the others on both her arms. They guided her slowly, while watching to maintain a good distance from Galena. Mrs. Vadoma and the little girl took a place with the freaks watching in the audience.

The mistress waved her hand, again, to summon Madame Fate back to their presence. Her machine flew in on the wind and landed to the left of the throne. She paused for a second then spoke aloud in foreign phrases even Mrs. Vadoma could not understand. Roughly translated the phrase was

"Reveal to me the law."

Madame Fate's eyes sprung open. Her head moved like a clock hand in the direction of the mistress. The crystal ball flashed a worn piece of paper. It wasn't a ticket since it was longer in size. It looked like a torn piece of paper from a book. Daniel and Mrs. Vadoma both knew which book it came from, to, (the *Montgomery, Cage House & Sideshow* book). With a snap of her fingers, the mistress summoned forth the book, which was also carried in by the wind. It hovered before the mistress then swiftly opened to the pages in which the laws were listed. Her eyes scrolled to the third law, which said: *No one may challenge the rule of the masters without just cause unless...* She took from Madame Fate the piece of paper to attach it to the missing part of the puzzle. Now the law mentioned: *No one may challenge the rule of the masters without just cause, unless they pass judgment before the Devil's Mistress.*

"Ah yes... Shall anyone here argue with the laws set down?" she glanced around her, seeing no brave soul raise his hand, "... very well. Clown, come forward." she demanded.

Charlie made his way, not even looking at the three as they were looking at him. By the way he presented himself, keeping that odious smile across that white-painted sorry excuse of a face, it seemed like Charlie was confident that everything was going to go his way in this obscene trial. He stood to the mistress's right side acting like an obedient dog as she began to say,

"Master Freak, Master Tamer, and Master Magician... the clown has accused you of neglecting that which has been given to you. He has shown me how you have abandoned the circus and are not worthy to possess your talents, which are only meant to maintain the circus."

"How could we have abandoned something that we had no idea we were responsible for?" Daniel demanded.

"Really, Master Magician? Did my sister not show you the past through your own eyes? And Master Freak and Master Tamer, did not your minions aid you and regale you with the truth about yourselves?"

"Look lady, Mistress, or Queen of Sheba for all I care!" Daniel intervened as she simply replied to his outburst with a raised eyebrow and a smile, "... we haven't done anything wrong, and besides, why are you listening to this last resort Joker for a Batman movie?"

"*FOOLISH BOY, CAN'T YOU SEE? THERE'S NO OTHER QUITE LIKE ME?*" exclaimed Charlie.

"Amusing Heir of Desmond; However, in your absence, it was the clown who took watch over the circus. And from what else I have seen you and your comrades have all used your powers outside of the grounds; which is also clearly mentioned in our laws as you can see here on the page,"

"What are you talking about?" CA asked.

Daniel received some of his flashes seconds after the mistress mentioned that they had been using powers not just in but also outside the Dark Circus. The flashes had shown him what she was referring. He could see himself practicing in the backyard with his cards and top hat. Then he could see Kyle painting his nails, throwing his voice, and wearing the old monster mask looking at himself in the mirror acting weird. In his flashes of CA, he could see the two German Sheppard dogs that belonged to Old Man Louise chasing her down an alley then turning on one another. Daniel realized that no matter what they said to prove their innocence they were guilty in this woman's eyes.

"*WHY SHOULD WE BOTHER, MISTRESS? THESE THREE ARE ALL TO BLAME. I'VE HAD ENOUGH, I TELL YOU, OF THIS FIDDLE-FADDLE GAME. I AM THE RIGHTFUL RULER... I AM ALL THERE SHOULD BE... NOW KEEP THE PROMISE MADE, AND GIVE THEIR POWER TO ME. WHO ELSE HERE IS WORTHY? WHO ELSE I SURELY ASK? I*

WANT MY RIGHTFUL DESTINY! I WANT TO FULLFIL THIS TASK!"

The mistress's eyes glowed the red shade she had displayed while raising the tent from the ground. It was enough to shut Charlie up fast and make him curl into a tiny ball below her feet. She soon bounced her focus back to the kids. Daniel's observation of this action caused his arm to go behind his back. He was gripping onto his trump, card so to speak, the card that morphs into a sword. He was getting it ready just in case she attempted to pull the same type of magic on them. Soon, Daniel had taken a bold risk by stepping forward.

"You're right, mistress."

C.A. and Daniel glanced at one another with expressions that seem to ask, *what the heck is he doing trying to get us all killed.*

"Go on." she said.

"We haven't been keeping up with our responsibilities to this place. To be honest, for the past three years, I have been trying to forget it ever happened. But now I know that by denying who we are and the things that we can do it only makes things worse. So, I would like to ask one thing from you before you decide what you want to do with us."

"Oh? What might that be young master?"

"That you let the others go and I will stay here to take the punishment."

Not one gasp of breath could be heard from C.A., Kyle, Mrs. Vadoma, the freaks, or even the lion (who was already struggling to breathe on account that he was split wide) open. Even the mistress seemed a bit surprised by this action.

"How noble, Heir of Desmond. Your ancestor was not this compassionate, especially when he stood by my side to decide who was fit to embrace the power of this kingdom. However, nobility aside, you were not alone in your ignorance."

C.A. was the first to rushed to his side.

"No, he wasn't," she said in a strong agreeable tone. "And he's not alone now."

Kyle went to the other side, also being the good friend and willing to take the punishment that was about to be rendered on them.

"What she said," Kyle said.

The mistress stared at the kids for a good while. The gang could feel right away that her judgment upon them would mean death. Was this the end of an interesting friendship? The time had finally come. She rose from her seat, gently closing the cover of the book. Her gaze never left their direction. She glided to Daniel, then stood before him like a statue. Her sweet lips formed a comforting smile. Charlie fearfully took notice of the silver torches. Their wild fire dimmed, making those in the audience get below the bleachers. The mistress's eyes glowed red, again.

She spun around sharply facing the clown.

"Charlie..." she smiled and threw her arms at the clown.

"*NO...NO...NO!*" the clown screamed.

The shape of the sleeves of her robes wrapped tightly around Charlie like a Christmas present. She slid to him like a chess piece, growing, towering, staggering above his frightened expression with yellow, sharp, jagged teeth protruding from her mouth. Now the three new why she was called the Devil's Mistress, because she was truly a demon and not of this world. Then she screamed with her voice echoing in two different tones throughout the tent

"Foul! Clown of the Dark Circus! I find you guilty of violating the law of the circus and corrupting its beauty to fit your own revenge! You are not worthy of the power *you* have been given by the magician's cape or by me! Desmond the Mystic took mercy on you by cutting your face, even his heir had taken mercy on you by feeding you to the lion you had murdered after I had freed you. But I, Clown.... will not be so merciful!"

The wind moved around the mistress and Charlie, forming a number five rated tornado. The two of them were sucked up through the round center of the tent's ceiling. The last sound they could hear from Charlie as he was being whisked away wasn't crying, as he probably should have been doing, but his laugh.

"*HAHAHAHAHAHAHAHAHAHAHAH AHAHAHAHAHAHAH!*"

Things were starting to deflate back into the earth, even the bleachers, torches, and the twisted throne. Mrs. Vadoma wasted no time.

She grabbed everyone she could get her hands on.

"Let's go now!"

They all made a swan dive through the burgundy curtains onto the hard pavement. They kept their heads tucked under their arms until they were sure things were okay. Daniel started to lift his head, followed by C.A., then Kyle, and so on.

Chapter 15
New Enemies Same Oak tree

WHAT COULD BE SAID about an astounding event like that? Charlie, the book, Madame Fate, and the Devil's Mistress. Everything should have returned to normal, and they should have all been flung away (back to the entrance of the empty lot), right? Well as someone once said, it isn't over till it's over.

In fact, the three young masters, their teacher, and the little girl were flung back to the gate. Unlike that last time when they defeated Charlie and were sent back to the other side where the oak tree stood, they were sent just out of the tent back on the same side of the lot where the carnival had been. They checked one another before taking another look at their surroundings. With cracks still in the pavement and stands knocked down and torn open, food, drinks, balloons, and everything else had been scattered everywhere. There was hardly a sound anymore (not even an owl hooting) that would indicate that a single soul had been up there tonight.

They took their time walking towards the gate altered itself back to normal. However, at the moment when they assumed that they were free to leave, who would show up to block the way, but Galena again.

"Ah! What do you want now?" Kyle fussed.

"Patience, young master... patience. You are not out of the woods, yet so they say. Not even you, my dear Trisha." she said in a teasing way.

"What more do you want from these children, Galena?"

"Careful... remember... what you have seen. I have spared you for now, Heir of Desmond."

"It must be my luckily day." Daniel responded.

"On the contrary, young masters. I have spared you all for two reasons. The first being that the early display of your powers (when you were attacked by the Charlie), impressed me. It also showed that you all might still have what it takes to continue on with the Dark Circus."

"What if we don't want to continue with it?" CA asked.

"That is a matter for another time. Secondly, as you may know, another harvest moon will be upon us."

"So?" Kyle shrugged his shoulders.

"The festival is at hand. It has been dormant for nearly a century, but now, I think it shall live again. Your teacher remembers the way to get there. By the law, you cannot refuse to come."

"You know, I'm getting sick and tired of hearing about these laws of yours." Daniel made a firm step.

She came closer to him, using her hand to brush the side of his cheek.

"The moon will be full in all her wonder. And you, Heir of Desmond, all of you, will have a final chance to prove yourselves not only to me, but to the crowds, just like in the olden days of glory. Then, Master Magician... you must make a choice between them... or you."

"Get away from me." Daniel shrugged her off.

She laughed inside her throat then continued to speak as she walked in the direction of Madame Fates Fortune Telling Machine, which had found its way from the fallen tent to behind Mrs. Vadoma.

"Be sure to bring your treasures with you when the time comes. Until we meet again."

The mistress stood by the machine. She took out the golden ticket from her black string necklace to put in the ticket slot of the machine. Then she pulled her robe's hood to cover the top half of her beautiful face. Near her feet and the bottom of the machine, another giant hole opened taking them deep down into the depths of the earth. After they vanished suddenly everyone was suddenly pushed out of the lot (by the forceful hand of the wind) to the outside of the gate where the police and ambulance attended to the other officers who were literally creamed by the pies.

The kids and Mrs. Vadoma assumed that their catapulted return to the front was going to attract more attention. But the officers that came up to them acted as if they had been standing there at the cars for a while.

"Come on, come on, there's nothing left for you all to see here."

"What happened, officer?" Mrs. Vadoma asked.

"Clearly, what went on here tonight was a well-planned out prank by one of the locals from Darby Town up the way. I tell you their jealousy about our giants going to the championship this year is eventually going to get them an all-day pass to County Jail if I have anything to say about it. Any ways, no more to see, come on everyone, back down to the town. And somebody get those kids away from that black tree over there. The roots are up, and it's not safe..."

Christy-Anne turned her attention to the black oak tree the officer was referring to, and she could see that it was Karl, Diana, and Andrew looking back at them.

"Hey guys look who it is." she told the boys who had also turned in the direction of the tree, "We'd better go get them before they get in trouble, too,"

"Hold on, C.A..." Kyle said with a concerned curiosity, "... I got to tell you guys something about those three."

But CA was already ahead of them. Daniel and Kyle soon quickly rushed after her while Mrs. Vadoma and the little girl went back down to the town as instructed.

Diana sat with her legs crossed on one of the large roots of the tree, petting and pressing against her cheek that silver snake bracelet. Andrew was also on one of the roots in a hunched position with his hair out, wearing the same wolf shirt and ripped pants that Kyle had seen him put on in the woods. Karl stood, leaning on one leg with his hands deep in his pockets. It was almost as if they were expecting Daniel and his friends to make it out of the Dark Circus alive. Now the plot thickens...

"Diana! Karl! What are you still doing up here?"

"Waiting for you," Diana spoke with a devious tone still petting her bracelet.

Daniel and Kyle could catch up; however, Kyle was trying to hint to Daniel about Andrew by clutching onto Daniel's arm

"*Houdini, I think we should get out of here!*" Kyle exclaimed in a whisper.

"What's wrong buddy?" Andrew intervened after eaves-dropping

"Yeah, what's wrong you guys?" C.A. said, turning her head back towards the boys

"Oh, he's probably just trying to tell your friend, Danny boy, here the truth about us." Karl removed his hands from his pockets to pull out more ping pong balls

"The truth? What do you mean the truth?" C.A. asked not having a clue.

"Hahaha, he's referring to is thisssssssssss...." Diana hissed. Roughly, she extended her arm with the bracelet attached to it towards C.A. The snakes that made up the bracelet untwisted and swirled forward on her hand to become live snake heads. The heads lunged with mouths wide open and fangs ready to bite down.

"WOW!" she screamed.

"C.A. look out!" Daniel yelled, running to her side.

Thankfully, C.A. was too fast for those things. She did a back flip that almost ended in a clumsy fall, but Daniel and Kyle were there to catch her arms. The snakes retracted quickly to Diana's arm, becoming a bracelet again. Andrew and Karl began to laugh.

"What the heck was that for?" CA shouted.

"Yeah, are you all out of your minds!" Daniel shouted moving in front of CA for her protection.

"Come on, man! Let me take them out with one shot." Andrew growled with each word.

"Easy, Wolfe. Don't forget about the festival." Karl signaled with one of his free hands.

"Festival? How do you know about that?" Daniel inquired.

"You think you're the only ones that went into the Dark Circus before? And read the book? There are creatures and people that have been involved with this thing for hundreds of years. Let me ask you something,

Master Magician. Do you remember the part in the story about your beloved ancestor, Desmond? It said that when Desmond was deciding who was fit to share the power of the Dark Circus, two were chosen out of the six. Did you ever ask yourselves who were the other four? One of them was that waste of air clown you took care of for us. The other three were our ancestors: Deedee Swartz, Alexander Cameron, and Klaus Utah. The Serpent, the Beast, and... the Juggler."

Kyle showed his ping pong balls which had been swirling on their own in his hand and were becoming the fire=balls he used earlier. He made them hover high seeming like he was going to take a toss, but it was just a psych out.

"You were right not to trust me, Daniel."

Karl quoted it exactly as Daniel remembered hearing it from his dreams.

"Karl. We have to go." Diana warned him, keeping a sharp eye out for the police who didn't seem to notice their little contest.

Karl smiled as he had turned off the fireworks. He shoved the ping pong balls back in his pockets. The full moon's bright glow was starting to fade with the night.

"The festival, masters. We'll see you at the festival. Let's go." Karl commanded his faithful sidekicks to follow him towards the road pass where the lighthouse once stood. Daniel and the others could see that in that direction was Karl's orange and black Dodge Challenger was in that direction, ready to take them away.

Now the kids had three new enemies to worry about. Soon, things started calming down as everyone went back to the town, not saying much for the first few minutes. Then they could hear, as they were coming closer to the center where the ice cream shop and the alley had been, people were still gathered around trying to celebrate what was left of the Halloween night., acting as if nothing had really happened. They could also hear that old violin and see the little gypsy girl bang on the tambourine of Mrs. Vadoma's song:

Come, sweet children, come with me... to a land of fear and fantasy... the land is magic, dark, and free... sweet children, won't you come with me

Mrs. Vadoma walked up to them wanting to say you did your best without sounding like some coach or motivational speaker. Instead she traded the use of comforting words for three caramel apples on a stick, which she handed them. She also tilted her head, signaling them to come over to join the last hour of the party. The trio looked at each other thinking, why not?

The clouds had rolled in and the moon was put to sleep... waiting for the next three years to fly by.

DEDICATION

I WOULD LIKE TO DEDICATE THIS BOOK TO MY ENTIRE FAMILY AND FRIENDS.

TO MY BELOVED GRANDFATHER, JAMES EVANS. HE WAS THE LOVE OF MY LIFE AND MY BEST FRIEND.

A SPECIAL THANK YOU TO <u>MICHELLE ANNE</u> FOR CREATING THE COVER ART FOR THIS BOOK

CPSIA information can be obtained
at www.ICGtesting.com
Printed in the USA
BVHW031925100619
550623BV00001B/63/P